## Also by Michelle Diener

*In a Treacherous Court*

*Dangerous Sanctuary* (ebook)

# KEEPER
# OF THE KING'S
# SECRETS

*a novel*

# MICHELLE DIENER

**G**

GALLERY BOOKS

NEW YORK   LONDON   TORONTO   SYDNEY   NEW DELHI

Gallery Books
A Division of Simon & Schuster, Inc.
1230 Avenue of the Americas
New York, NY 10020

This book is a work of fiction. Names, characters, places, and incidents either are products of the author's imagination or are used fictitiously. Any resemblance to actual events or locales or persons, living or dead, is entirely coincidental.

First Gallery Books paperback edition April 2012

GALLERY BOOKS and colophon are trademarks of Simon & Schuster, Inc.

For information about special discounts for bulk purchases, please contact Simon & Schuster Special Sales at 1-866-506-1949 or business@simonandschuster.com.

The Simon & Schuster Speakers Bureau can bring authors to your live event. For more information or to book an event, contact the Simon & Schuster Speakers Bureau at 1-866-248-3049 or visit our website at www.simonspeakers.com.

Library of Congress Cataloging-in-Publication Data
  Diener, Michele.
    Keeper of the king's secrets / Michelle Diener. — 1st Gallery Books paperback ed.
      p. cm.
    1. Great Britain—History—Henry VIII, 1509-1547—Fiction. 2. Courts and courtiers—Fiction. I. Title. PR9619.4.D54K44 2012          2011028892
823'.92—dc23

Designed by Jaime Putorti

Manufactured in the United States of America

10  9  8  7  6  5  4  3  2  1

ISBN 978-1-4391-9709-7
ISBN 978-1-4391-9711-0 (ebook)

*To Liz—an inspiration and a hero*

# ACKNOWLEDGMENTS

A huge thank-you to Marlene Stringer and Micki Nuding. You are the most wonderful and supportive agent and editor a writer could wish for. Thank you as well to the amazing team at Simon & Schuster, including Parisa Zolfaghari, Lisa Litwack and her team, Tom Pitoniak, Jaime Putorti, Ayelet Gruenspecht, Jean Anne Rose, and the many others who work in production, sales, and marketing. You are all amazing and there aren't enough Tim Tams in existence to shower you with as you deserve!

Liz Kreger and Edie Ramer helped me weed out the errors in the first draft, and many other friends gave me support and encouragement. Thank you.

And last, but not least, to my children and husband for the love and support you give me.

# 1

*Upon this, one has to remark that men ought either to be well treated or crushed, because they can avenge themselves of lighter injuries, of more serious ones they cannot; therefore the injury that is to be done to a man ought to be of such a kind that one does not stand in fear of revenge.*

—Niccolò Machiavelli, The Prince, *chapter 4 (translated by* W. K. Marriott)

Upper Thames Street was crowded as Londoners took advantage of the first warm day of the new year. Susanna cradled her purchases like a baby in front of her, keeping a good hold on the satchel's strap. Gold leaf required delicate handling.

The street was full of shops run by merchants from the Netherlands, France, and Italy, and she alternated between watching her footing in the March mud and searching the display of wares set out to attract the eye for lapis lazuli. She hadn't been able to get enough of it earlier.

Perhaps because she was looking for blue, she noticed the man in the deep blue cloak stepping out of a jeweller's shop. Something in the turn of his head, the jut of his jaw, was familiar, and she moved closer to get a better look.

"Master Jens?" she called in English; then she called his name again in her native Flemish.

He checked his step, turned, and seemed to jerk back at the sight of her—but that could not be right. He must have tripped on something or slipped in the mud.

Susanna waved as best she could without loosening her hold on her bag.

He turned away, unseeing. Only she could have sworn he had seen her. It must be that he didn't know she was living in London now, and thought his eyes were playing tricks on him.

"Master Jens, it's Susanna Horenbout!" Her call cut through the street noise, and she ran after him.

As he turned into a narrow alleyway her hand grasped his cloak, and he surprised her with a sharp cry of fear.

"Master Jens." She smiled at him as he turned; he must have thought her some brigand. "I did not mean to startle you. I could hardly believe my eyes when I saw you come out of that jeweller's shop. It makes my heart glad to see a familiar face."

"Susanna." He tried to smile back, but it was a sick thing, forced at the corners and white-edged.

"Are you ill?" Susanna frowned. Her hand came up to feel his forehead, then stopped in a strange salute as he cringed back from her into deep shadow.

She noticed now that the alley was barely more than a rank passageway, and what little sunlight managed to angle itself into the narrow space stopped high on the left-hand wall.

"Master Jens, what is wrong?" She wanted to back out into

the light and bustle of the street, but family ties and respect forced her to take another step toward her father's friend.

He drew back farther into the gloom. "Nothing, nothing. Just a touch of travel fever."

His voice sounded more like his own, this time, and Susanna relaxed. "If you come home with me, I'll call our local healer to see to you. I can vouch for her knowledge. We can dine and exchange news."

"I'm afraid that won't be possible." He seemed to fold in on himself, sinking to the ground, and Susanna bridged the distance between them in two strides, then knelt beside him.

She felt his forehead, which was cool and dry. She tried to see his face in the shadows, shifting so she didn't block all the light.

His eyes shocked her, filled with the terror and rage of a trapped animal.

She fell back with a cry as his arm swung up and over. She scrambled back and heard a crunch as whatever was in his hand became buried in the earthen alleyway floor.

He pulled it out, lifted it up again, and she saw it was a chisel, dark-edged and finely honed. His diamond-cleaving chisel.

She struggled to find her feet, hopelessly entangled in her gown. He moved toward her on his knees, chisel raised, like some mad cleric sacrificing to a vengeful god.

He wanted her dead.

Susanna thought of Parker, her betrothed's face coming to her clear and sharp, and she flicked her arm. The knife he'd given her dropped into her palm and then Jens was on her, swinging wildly.

There was a sharp sting where her neck met her shoulder, and she lunged forward. Felt the brief resistance, then the give as her blade found its mark.

Jens reared back, her blood dripping from his weapon, her knife embedded high on his right side, just below his shoulder.

He stared down at the blade, buried hilt-deep, his breath coming in short, sharp gasps. He fumbled for the wall, pulled himself up. Once he was standing, he looked down on her with eyes glazed over in shock.

His fingers shook as he tried to push his chisel into the leather pouch on his belt. He couldn't make it go in, and dropped it to the ground, stumbling past her, the blade still protruding, a strange keening coming from his throat, his movements jerky and uncoordinated as he staggered away.

Susanna realized her own breathing was too shallow, and she forced herself to hold her breath, to let it out slowly, then draw in a deep gulp of air.

The chisel lay in front of her, bloodstained, mud-stained. Sharp enough to cut diamonds. She shuddered and fought down the sob that rose in her throat. Her hand closed over it and she slipped it into her pocket.

She got slowly, stiffly, to her feet and picked up her satchel. She could feel the trickle of blood running into the groove of her collarbone and then down between her breasts.

Master Jens was one of her father's best friends. He'd stayed at their home many times, had bounced her on his knee when she was small.

An icy ball of fear and confusion sat in her stomach, and she breathed deep again to keep herself from heaving her breakfast onto the ground.

Then she limped out of the alleyway, finally feeling the scrapes on her knees.

She needed to get home.

---

Anyone watching Dr. Pettigrew wind his way through the stalls on London Bridge would see a man of wealth going about his business. Parker saw nothing but a stone-cold killer.

He followed Pettigrew stealthily, the shock of spotting the doctor shuddering through him. That Pettigrew had come to London, within half a mile of Parker's house, set a slow fire burning in his gut.

He ignored the shouts of the market, the pushing crowds, as he kept Pettigrew in sight.

The doctor slowed, glancing at the buildings on the upstream side of the bridge.

A man stood within the doorway of one of the houses, his face in shadow, and Parker saw the moment the two made eye contact. Pettigrew relaxed, hitched the leather bag on his shoulder higher, and stepped into the house.

The door swung shut behind him.

Parker looked for a place to wait. Pettigrew had to come out the way he went in. There were no back doors in the houses built on either side of London Bridge—unless you were prepared to swim.

Pettigrew worked for the Duke of Norfolk, and anything Norfolk was up to was of interest to Parker. He and the Duke had been forced to come to an uneasy truce a month ago, but Parker didn't trust the Duke not to renege on the bargain they had struck, or start new trouble.

Someone jostled him, bumping his elbow, and Parker snaked out a hand and grabbed the small boy trying to duck past him.

For a moment the boy's gaze locked with his own, and Parker saw the cockiness, and the cunning, die in his eyes.

The boy shivered. "I didn't steal nothing."

Parker suppressed the urge to hand over a coin at the sight of his pinched face, drawn tight with hunger. When he'd been on the street like this, he'd have taken that kind of gesture as a sign of weakness. "I know."

The boy stared at Parker's hand, still gripping his arm. "Well?"

"What do you know about that house?" Parker jerked his head and pulled a coin from his bag.

"Foreigners live there." The boy pulled himself taller. "Rich 'n' all." He eyed the money.

"Where're they from?" Parker did not loosen his hold.

The boy tried to yank his arm away but gave up when he realized there was no give. "Foreigners is foreigners. I don't know."

Parker flicked the coin at him and let him go, and the boy caught it neatly, then dived into the crowd.

Parker gazed thoughtfully at the house. Foreigners.

The last time he'd had dealings with Pettigrew, the doctor was on a ship from Ghent. The ship that had brought Susanna to England. What new plot from the Continent was Norfolk involved in now?

Before he could ponder the question, Pettigrew stepped out of the house. Parker turned to face a stall as the doctor swung left, back the way he'd come.

He could come back later and find out who lived here, so Parker followed Pettigrew. He wanted to make sure Norfolk's hand was in this. There was a small possibility that this was Pettigrew's private business.

He slipped into the crowds and walked easily in Pettigrew's wake.

# 2

*. . . a man who wishes to act entirely up to his profes-
sions of virtue soon meets with what destroys him
among so much that is evil.*

—Machiavelli, The Prince, chapter 15

Maggie was the first sign that something was wrong. The healer was coming out of Crooked Lane, and Parker frowned at the sight of her.

She looked up, and pity or concern flashed in her eyes. There could be only one reason for it—only one thing meant anything to him.

He ran toward her.

"She was lucky." Maggie looked straight at him, one of the few who had the nerve to do so when he felt like this, like an icy storm raged inside him. "Just a scratch really, and her knees aren't bad. She'd get as much from slipping in this cursed mud."

He had enough civility in him to lift a hand in salute, but

he could feel it unraveling as he raced for his front door, leaving nothing but the wild core of him exposed.

The door opened before he reached it and Mistress Greene jerked her head toward the study.

"She wouldn't go to bed, but she's resting by the fire."

He gave a nod and moved past her, something easing a little within him. If Susanna was refusing bed, she wasn't at death's door.

He stepped into the room and stared at her, curled in her usual chair. His betrothed's hair was always dressed and under a cap, but now the cap had been removed and the heavy, dark mass was piled almost on top of her head, to keep it away from her neck.

Away from the deep, angry gash in her pale skin.

"Who did this, did you see them?" He held himself back from her, afraid to touch her with the rage burning so hot inside him. His hands were white-knuckled fists.

"I stabbed him." She drew in a shaky breath, her eyes wide as she looked at him. "With the knife you gave me. It was still stuck in his chest when he ran off."

He blinked. "Good."

"Parker, I cannot believe he would do this. I cannot believe it even happened. If this wasn't here"—she lifted fingers to her neck—"if I didn't still have the chisel he stabbed me with, I would be trying to convince myself it was a nightmare."

"You *know* who did this?"

Susanna nodded. "Master Jens of Antwerp. He's a *diaman-*

*taire*, a diamond cutter. He's been my father's friend since they were apprentices."

Parker fell to his knees beside her, took her hands in his. Whatever he'd thought, whatever he'd expected, this was not it. "Why would he attack you?"

She shook her head. "He pretended not to see me, and ducked into an alley. As if he didn't want me drawing attention to him." She stroked her thumbs along the sides of his palms.

"Perhaps he didn't want to be recognized." Parker frowned. "He may have been afraid you would write home and mention you had seen him here."

Susanna laced her fingers with his. "If he were here in secret, my seeing him would have ruined his plans. But what secret is so big, he'd kill the daughter of one of his oldest friends to keep it that way?"

Parker thought back to Pettigrew, to how trouble from the Low Countries seemed to follow in his wake. Parker had followed him straight back to the Duke of Norfolk's quarters, and knew where to start his inquiries.

He smoothed his hand down the back of her neck, careful not to hurt her, then kissed her forehead. "We'll find out. But there is something I have to do before I go out and ask questions." He rose, and she tipped her head back to look at him.

"What?"

"Get you another knife."

There was a deep eave over Norfolk's door, and Susanna shivered in the cold gloom, pulling her cape tighter about her.

Parker leaned forward and hammered on the door again.

At last they heard the shuffle of footsteps, and the clink and rattle of keys.

As the door swung inward, Parker gave it a shove and Norfolk's man stumbled back. He looked more like a stable-hand than a servant. No wonder there had been a delay in opening the door. When Norfolk had realized who was knocking, he'd gone to find one of his thugs to welcome them.

Susanna saw the servant's eyes flick from Parker's chain of office, a mark of how high he stood in favor with the King, to his face. The servant took a step back, his gaze moving to the right.

"Parker." Norfolk stepped from the shadows of a passage-way with a cold smile. He appeared relaxed, leaning against a door frame, but Susanna noticed his hand gripped the wood instead of resting against it.

She hadn't seen him since the service at St. Paul's. The King had arranged the ceremony to give thanks to God for the death of his rival for the throne, Richard de la Pole. The fact that Norfolk had been conspiring with de la Pole, and that she and Parker had uncovered that conspiracy, even though their hands were tied over exposing the Duke, had made that meeting colder than the freezing air of the cathedral.

The atmosphere was no warmer now.

Parker took a step forward, and the color drained from Norfolk's face. His smile wavered, then he gathered himself and gave a curt nod.

"We'll talk in my study." He made a motion to the servant, and the man melted back into the shadows of the hall.

Norfolk preceded them down the passage a little way and turned into a room. Susanna knew it must have cost him to turn his back on Parker.

Parker closed the door behind them, and Norfolk spun as it thumped shut, then sank slowly into his chair. "What is it you think I've done?" He forced his hands still by laying them on his desk.

"Draw back your cape," Parker commanded.

Susanna lifted the heavy velvet hood off her head, and untied her cloak at the neck to reveal her wound.

Norfolk started, and Susanna had the feeling it was in relief. "That wasn't me." Norfolk's eyes did not leave her.

"I'm not suggesting you did this with your own hands." Parker had not raised his voice, but Norfolk's gaze moved to him.

"It was not on my orders, either."

"Sometimes your orders are rather . . . vague." Parker drew her cloak closed. "And we know you tried to kill my lady before."

Norfolk's nostrils pinched as he drew in a breath. He tilted his head. "I tell you, I had no part in this."

Susanna looked at him, at the deep lines of discontent and arrogance defining his face, and believed him. "Do you know a diamond cutter, Jens of Antwerp?"

He seemed startled that she'd spoken.

"Diamonds?" Norfolk asked slowly, drawing the word out as if stalling.

"We are not talking about diamonds." Parker's voice betrayed no hint he had noticed Norfolk's reaction. "We are talking about diamond cutters. And whether you have one in your employ named Jens of Antwerp."

"I do not." Norfolk had hold of himself again, and he stroked his chin. "Was that who attacked Mistress Horenbout?"

Parker didn't answer the question. He stepped back and opened the door, holding his arm out for Susanna to take.

She didn't curtsy to Norfolk or even nod farewell, despite his being the highest-ranking nobleman in England aside from the King.

"I see the good doctor Pettigrew is in town," Parker said, and she froze mid-step across the threshold, glad Norfolk couldn't see the surprise on her face. Pettigrew was back?

Norfolk spluttered and she glanced over her shoulder, and saw he had gone pale for the second time since they'd arrived.

"You can tell him, especially after the attack on Susanna today, that if he sets foot in Cheapside again, he will not come out alive." Parker did not wait for Norfolk's response as he stepped into the hall with her.

"Parker, that business is finished. You, your lady, and I, we have an agreement. I will abide by my end, you by yours. Pettigrew is no longer a danger to either of you."

Parker gave him one last look. "Pettigrew may be no danger to me, or to Mistress Horenbout, but you can be sure if he comes to my side of London again, I will be a danger to him."

# 3

*For, although one may be very strong in armed forces,
yet in entering a province one has always need of the
goodwill of the natives.*

—Machiavelli, The Prince, *chapter 3*

Harry's boys had done well to track Jens down so fast.

Parker stood deep in shadow at the back door of the inn, forcing himself to be still, though the chill night air made him want to move about for warmth.

The building stood at a crossroads. Carts and travelers had been coming and going through the early evening, but things were quiet on the road now.

The only noise came from the tavern. Someone had started up on a lute, and the sound of singing, clapping, and stomping filtered out into the crisp night.

The inn was a good place to hide. No one would notice a traveler here, especially if he took a private room and kept to himself.

Master Jens might have managed it—except he'd returned this afternoon with a knife wound. Even in London, that was something to be remarked upon.

The back door creaked and a shadow slipped out, then hesitated a moment.

Parker noted his spy's stealth with approval. Harry had not been working for him long, but he'd proved himself in that business with Norfolk a month ago. He'd proved himself again today by finding Jens so quickly.

Parker stepped forward. "What do you have?"

Harry put a hand to his heart. "You move too quiet for someone so big." His voice quavered and he cleared his throat. "Our man is in his room. He had a visitor 'bout twenty minutes ago. He was up there less than ten minutes 'fore he came back down."

Parker could smell the hops on Harry's breath. "Had a mug, did you?"

In the weak light seeping from the shuttered inn windows, Parker saw him grin. "Had to blend in."

"As long as it doesn't slow you down."

"We're going up?"

"I am." Parker scanned the back courtyard. "You keep watch downstairs." He tucked his cloak behind his sword. "There a servant's way up?"

Harry nodded. "Go left when we're inside. You won't need to go through the main tavern to get upstairs."

Parker opened the door and held it as Harry slipped past, then stepped into the narrow passage after him. Laughter and the clink of cups came from a large room to the right, and Parker took the dimly lit way to the left, leaving Harry to slip back into the taproom.

He could smell the rich, dark flavor of stew and the sharp sourness of beer as he came to a steep staircase.

He climbed it swiftly, without worrying about creaking wooden boards or the sound of his footsteps.

He already knew which room Jens had taken, had been watching it from below. With the shutters drawn, he'd only been able to see the weak glow of candlelight from within.

He went straight to the door, tapped it lightly, then stood back. His hand went to his sword and he began to draw it from its scabbard.

Without warning, the door was flung open. Parker leaped back, his sword coming up.

The man rushing from the room had his head down, a hat drawn low over his face.

He came on fast, dodged Parker, and leaped down the stairs, swearing as he slipped and half-fell the rest of the way. Parker heard the drum of the man's boots as he ran down the passageway, then the slam of the back door as it was flung open.

Parker kept his sword in hand. He had to choose, and he chose Jens.

He stepped into the room, sword up and center. The only person within lay on a bed pushed against the far wall. His eyes glittered in the candlelight, his hands pawing at his neck, and Parker moved closer.

Jens flinched back and drew in a rattling, wheezing breath. There was a garrote around his neck, which he'd loosened enough to give him precious air, and Parker grabbed the twine and pulled it wider, allowing him a full, deep breath.

There were scratches on the diamond cutter's neck along with a deep, angry welt. Blood stained his nails where he'd fought to loosen the garrote's hold. He lifted his hands, scrabbling at Parker's chest as if to keep him off. His mouth opened and closed like a fish as he choked and whooped, fighting air into his lungs.

Parker turned back to the door. The assassin had failed, and he must know it.

If he were a professional, he would try again. Soon, before Jens could talk.

Parker had been prepared to kill him himself—but this murder attempt showed clearly that Jens was not the only one who would kill to keep his presence in London secret.

Parker needed more information.

He glanced about the room. There was a large traveling bag on the floor, and a small satchel on a desk. Parker grabbed them both.

He risked turning his back on the door for a moment to haul Jens upright and pull him from the bed.

Jens resisted, twisting in his arms.

"I'm taking you somewhere safe." Parker tightened his grip. "If I wanted you dead, you'd be dead."

Jens was still gulping in air, but he relaxed, let Parker set him on his feet and steady him with an arm.

Where in damnation was Harry?

He didn't want to step out of the room with only one hand free, and the weight of a man and two bags on his other arm.

There was a sound of running feet from the main stairs, and Parker dumped Jens back on the bed. He dropped the bags and raised his sword with one arm, flicked the other arm, and felt the cool hilt of his knife drop into his palm.

It was Harry, breathing hard. "Tried to follow him, but he disappeared about ten paces outside the inn. He could have gone anywhere, and I guessed you might need me here."

Parker jerked his head toward the diamond cutter. "Help him down the back stairs. I'll make sure there are no more surprises."

He picked up the bags and went ahead, listening first, then gesturing to Harry to bring Jens down. Harry had grown in the last month, but he was still slight and thin from years of starving on the streets, so his progress with the injured man was slow.

At last they reached the back door. Parker held it open, the hairs on the back of his neck prickling as he waited for Harry. They were exposed, with the light from within the tavern making them a perfect target.

"Fast as you can." He forced the impatience from his voice as Harry moved past him, breathing hard under Jens's heavy weight.

There was a tiny scrape of metal on metal, and Parker instantly pulled Harry down, jerking him out from under Jens's arm.

Jens fell with a cry as Parker pushed Harry into the shadows, his eyes straining for any sign of the assassin in the darkness of the yard.

To his left, Jens convulsed, and Parker saw a crossbow bolt protruding from his throat. The diamond cutter fought an impossible battle for air, then lay still.

In the sudden silence, Parker heard movement and braced for another bolt, but the only sound was of boots running on cobbles, fading into the night. Parker could hear an uneven cadence to the step: a limp. The assassin had hurt himself in his tumble down the stairs.

"I thought he'd run off the first time." Harry emerged trembling from the dark corner where Parker had pushed him.

"He hadn't finished the job." Parker stood and went over to Jens's body. The man's eyes were lifeless, staring up into the cold, clear night.

He crouched down to study the bolt sticking out of Jens's throat. The wooden shaft was well made, the metal tip buried too deep to be visible.

It was a master shot.

"How did he slip past us to get in that room to begin with?" Harry flicked a glance at Jens, and then away.

Parker rose up. "He must have been watching you. Went up when you came to report to me."

Harry looked like he wanted to be sick. "I didn't notice anyone."

Parker moved out into the courtyard and Harry followed him. "What will we do with the body?"

Parker glanced back at Jens, crumpled against the back door. "Leave it where it is. We have to find the other man you saw going up to Jens's room. And visit the jeweller's shop Susanna saw Jens leaving yesterday."

Harry looked at him sharply. "What about the assassin?"

"If Jens had a secret someone wants to bury, then anyone who had contact with Jens before he died is in danger. If we find them first, the assassin will come to us." Parker led the way down a short alley, to where they'd left their horses. "At least we know a few things."

"We don't know anything." Harry untied the mounts with sharp, frustrated tugs. "We didn't even see his face."

Parker sheathed his sword. "When he fell down the stairs after I'd interrupted him with Jens, he swore in French."

He slipped a foot into the stirrup and pulled himself up.

"A Frenchman! You really think he'll go after whoever had contact with Jens?"

Parker nodded.

"But that means . . ." Harry couldn't finish the sentence.

Parker did it for him, as he forced his mount into a canter. "Susanna is in this bastard's sights."

# 4

*But when states are acquired in a country differing in
language, customs, or laws, there are difficulties, and
good fortune and great energy are needed to hold them,
and one of the greatest and most real helps would be that
he who has acquired them should go and reside there.*

—Machiavelli, The Prince, *chapter 4*

arker's face was grim. Dark shadows clung to him as he
stepped into the hallway, and Susanna drew him into the
study, into the warm glow of the fire.

"Harry?" she asked.

"In the stables, helping Eric and Peter Jack see to the
horses."

"And Master Jens?"

"Dead." He looked straight at her as he spoke.

Jens had tried to kill her, but she could not link the wild-
eyed man in the alley to the man she had known. The man
she had respected and liked. She felt a strange sense of confusion. She did not know what to do with her hands, with any
part of herself.

Parker's gaze rested on her, and she had the sense that he wanted to draw her to him but didn't know if she would accept his touch. "His death was not by my hand. Someone wanted him silent."

She lifted her hands to his cloak, undid the tie, and drew it off his shoulders. At last he slid his hands along her arms, pulled her close. They stood, quiet, peaceful, and she closed her eyes, leaning into him.

When she stepped back, he took his cloak from her and draped it over a chair, his face lighter than when he'd come in.

She should paint him like this. Standing by the firelight, dressed in unrelenting black, his black hair gleaming. There was something in the way he carried himself, a readiness for action, that would be a challenge to capture.

"You will mourn him?" He walked to the windows and checked that the shutters were fast.

"I will. I don't know what I will say to my parents." She rubbed at her temples. There were plenty of things she did not know how to say to her parents. Her presence in Parker's house being one. Her presence in his bed another.

Her parents had sent her to Henry's court to separate her from a man they thought unsuitable, and to paint for the English king, and already she had found a betrothed, been drawn into court intrigue, and made an enemy of the Duke of Norfolk. Her father would bring her home if he knew but the half of it.

As if he could read her thoughts, Parker turned. "Have you told them of our betrothal?"

She nodded. "I have. I want to give them as much time as possible to make plans to attend the wedding. I expect a reply soon—if they're still talking to me."

Parker's grin lit his face and pierced her heart. He was beautiful when he smiled. "You're marrying a king's courtier. Surely that is better than the illicit liaison with a blacksmith your parents sent you to England to prevent?"

She snorted. "I don't think my father will see it that way when he learns I'm living with you already."

Parker raised an eyebrow. "They do not know that?"

She shook her head.

"I could offer to send you to my home in Fulham. But in truth, I want no such thing." He bridged the small distance between them, put his hands on her shoulders. "I want you close, Susanna. Close as you can be."

A feather-brush of warmth, of delight, stroked across her skin at his words. Who would have guessed this journey to London had not been into exile, as she first thought, but a chance to find a love she never dared hope for?

Parker's eyes slid to the shutters. "If the man who killed Jens learns you saw Jens this morning and spoke with him, you could be his next target."

She went still. "How could he learn of it?"

"Jens could have talked." Parker shrugged. "He could have been following Jens this morning, come to that."

"What was Jens involved with? Why would he risk everything, even his life, for it?"

Parker's gaze hardened. "Whatever it is, Norfolk is involved somehow—which means there is some advantage in it for him."

Susanna recalled the shock in Norfolk's eyes. "When I said 'diamond cutter,' he almost lost his composure."

"Aye." This time Parker's grin did not light his face. "I will put Harry on to watching him. The fastest way to uncover this mystery may be to find out what Norfolk is up to. He may lead us to Jens's killer."

"And Pettigrew?" She shivered at the thought of the doctor lurking somewhere in the city, malevolent and dangerous.

Parker drew back from her. "I think Norfolk understood me. I don't think we'll be seeing the doctor again."

———————

Parker slowed, and looked up. The jeweller's well-appointed shop had a carved sign hanging above the door, and was raised from the street by wooden stairs and a small platform. The proprietor was doing well.

Instead of going within, Parker walked past the shop without so much as looking in the window, and turned into the mean alleyway where Jens had tried to kill Susanna.

The fine lace of his shirt cuff caught on the rough stone of the alley wall, and he jerked it free. There was almost nothing here to show what had happened yesterday. Only a smudge of blood on the wall.

The answers to this lay elsewhere, some of them in the little shop around the corner.

He swung back into the street, climbed the few stairs, and pushed on the door, and it opened with a tinkle of a bell. He had half expected the place to be locked up.

The jeweller came out from the back, wiping his hands on a cloth that glinted with gold dust. A man who worked and fashioned jewelry, then, instead of just selling it.

He took in Parker's fine clothes, but when he noted the chain of office under Parker's cloak, instead of smiling with satisfaction at having an important paying customer, fear flared in his eyes.

"Yes?" He spoke as if struggling for breath. He edged a step closer to the door to his workshop.

Parker chose the direct approach. "You had a visitor to your shop yesterday, Jens of Antwerp. What did he want?"

"Who would be asking, sir?" The jeweller tried to keep his voice firm.

"I'm the Keeper of the Palace of Westminster, and the King's Yeoman of the Crossbows." Parker pulled his cloak back for the man to see the chain more clearly.

He paled at the list of Parker's offices, and his eyes darted about his shop, refusing to alight on Parker's face. "I have many visitors every day, and not all give me their name."

"This man wore a blue cloak and was a diamond cutter from Antwerp. As a fellow professional, it would be strange if you had not exchanged names."

The jeweller opened his mouth, as if to answer, then bolted to his back room. He was short and round, and Parker leaped over the counter and caught hold of the back of the man's doublet before he had taken more than three steps.

"Unhand me, sir. I know nothing. Nothing." His voice quavered. His body shook with fear.

"You can answer me here, privately, and we could leave it at that, or you could come with me to the Tower." Parker kept his hold firm. "What will it be?"

"Pr . . . privately?" The jeweller's tone held a sliver of hope.

"Aye."

He slumped and Parker released him, let him turn and press himself up against the wall.

"In truth, I do not know much. Jens is an acquaintance. He is one of the finest diamond cutters in the world, and I have sent gems to him for cutting before. He said only that he was in dire trouble, and had no more funds. He needed to catch a ship back to Antwerp, and I guessed the trouble was serious."

He lifted his hands helplessly. "I lent him the coin he asked for. He promised to pay me back and I had no cause to mistrust him, but something about him . . ." The man shuddered. "He was almost wild with fear, muttering about the Tower. So perhaps, as a loyal Englishman, I should not have lent him that money." The jeweller looked up at Parker, resignation in the lines of his face.

"You helped a friend, and you did not know the nature of his trouble." And neither did he, Parker thought, his mood sour. This was a dead end.

"I am not in trouble?"

Parker shook his head. "Not with the King. But Jens is dead, and I have a feeling that if his visit here yesterday becomes known, you may suffer the same fate. If you have a place to go for a week or more, I would suggest you take yourself off."

Parker left him throwing things into a bag and stepped out into the street.

From the corner of his eye, he noticed a man push himself off the wall he was leaning against and walk away, a slight limp to his step.

Parker had told Harry that if they tracked down all the people Jens had seen on his last day, the assassin would come to them, but he had known his chances were slight. Now every nerve tingled.

Without breaking stride, he turned in the same direction, his heart pounding in anticipation. If this was the assassin, he finally had a chance to get some answers.

# 5

*A wise man ought always to follow the paths beaten by great men, and to imitate those who have been supreme, so that if his ability does not equal theirs, at least it will savour of it.*

—Machiavelli, The Prince, *chapter 6*

Parker had said not to leave the house, but he hadn't counted on a summons from the King. Susanna added parchment and quills to her leather satchel and ignored the frown on Peter Jack's face.

Simon lifted his hands in supplication at the look Peter Jack sent him. "The King wants her immediately." He was so easygoing, so good-natured, Susanna suspected the King used him whenever the delivery or the tidings were unlikely to make anyone happy. But she knew firsthand he could be counted on. He'd come to her aid often enough since she'd arrived in England and he'd driven her from Dover to London in his capacity as the King's official transporter.

"I thought the King was away in the country, hawking." Peter Jack crossed his arms over his chest, and Susanna noticed they were bigger, more muscled than they had been a month ago, when he'd been a child on the streets.

"He is." Simon took her satchel and gave a startled "oomph" at its weight.

"Then how can he want her immediately?"

"He wants her to illuminate a document he sent me to deliver to Cardinal Wolsey. The Cardinal is impatient to send it off, but cannot until Susanna has done her work."

Susanna stepped around Peter Jack, toward the door. "And it *is* my work, what I was brought to London to do."

Simon stepped around Peter Jack as well. From the corner of her eye, Susanna saw him tug gently at Peter Jack's ear. "Well, are you coming, or will you stand there glowering until we get back?"

"I'm coming." Peter Jack's words were stiff.

Susanna turned to soothe his worry, knowing he blamed himself for not being with her when she was attacked, and caught him sliding a knife up his sleeve. She gaped. Did Parker have them all doing it?

He caught her shocked expression. "Can't protect you with my bare hands. Or not as well." He straightened, and Susanna could see an edge of steel in the set of his shoulders. He looked older than his fifteen years now—sure and confident, where before he'd looked frail and fragile, with old, old eyes.

She wondered if his eyes would ever lose that look.

"I hope you won't have to protect me at all, but it is good you're coming. Parker won't have cause to be as cross." She looked over to Simon, who was waiting impatiently at the door. "Can you tell Mistress Greene which part of the palace I will be in, so Parker knows how to find us?"

"Aye." He clamped his jaw down with a sharp click, then turned down the passage to the kitchen. As she and Peter Jack followed behind him, she heard him speaking easily enough to Parker's housekeeper.

"Thought you weren't to go anywhere." Mistress Greene's mouth was a thin line.

"Order of the King." Susanna shrugged. "I know he'll be furious, but what can I do?"

"Nothing. And time is wasting." Simon went to the back door and held it open.

"I'll tell the master." Mistress Greene picked up her bread dough and slapped it hard on the counter. "Though I hope you get back before he does."

Susanna lifted a hand to her neck and smoothed the cut with uneasy fingers. "That would be best, but it won't happen if I'm to do the illumination at the Cardinal's office." She darted a quick look at Simon, and he nodded confirmation. "Then I'll be back late."

Simon gave a meaningful sweep of his arm.

"I'm coming." She looked across at Peter Jack. "Ready?"

He nodded. "I'd rather face whoever is out there than Parker when he finds us both gone."

"'Tis me and Eric'll have to face him." Mistress Greene

looked to the door just as Eric slipped under Simon's arm, coming in from the backyard.

"Face who?"

"She's leaving the house," Peter Jack told his younger brother.

"Oh?" Eric rubbed the back of his head. "Oh!" He looked over at Simon. "Can I come, too?"

"No, you don't. I'm not facing him alone." Mistress Greene worked the dough.

"For heaven's sake. It is by order of the King." Susanna went to the door. "Parker will understand. He would do the same."

She took the steps down into the yard, hoping she was right.

# 6

*And it has always been the opinion and judgment of*
*wise men that nothing can be so uncertain or unstable*
*as fame or power not founded on its own strength.*

—Machiavelli, The Prince, *chapter 13*

"Mistress Horenbout." Cardinal Wolsey's nod was curt as Simon ushered her into his office and announced her. The Cardinal's eyes were fish-cold and as fathomless, and she suppressed a shiver.

"Your Grace." She curtsied deeply and saw his hand clench with impatience.

"This missive must go out as soon as you are done. Can I impress upon you, madame, that in this case it is better to have a simple, elegant drawing than an intricate one?" He indicated a sloped, empty desk near the window, and she liked the way the light fell on it to the left, so her hand would not cast a shadow on her work. It would do nicely.

It was past midday, but she would have a good few hours of daylight left.

She held out her hand to Simon for her satchel, then hefted it onto the table.

The Cardinal flicked the back of his hand at Simon. "Be gone."

With a regretful quirk of his lips, Simon backed out of the room. As he closed the door, Susanna saw Peter Jack peering in for a quick look at the Cardinal's chambers.

She smiled. The thick, luxurious carpets from Turkey, the jewel-colored wall hangings, and the gleaming wood furniture would not have disappointed him. She had been in the King's closet in this same palace, and she would say the Cardinal's had cost more to furnish than the King's.

She set about lining her pigments along the top of the desk, setting out her clean mussel shells for mixing, then took out her pencils, pens, and scrapers. She looked across at the Cardinal expectantly.

He picked the missive up, and then set it down again as if changing his mind about giving it to her.

She kept her face impassive.

He looked across at her, and then slowly lifted the thick roll of parchment again and held it out to her. "Here."

She rose and took it before he could snatch it back; then she sat down and rolled it out carefully. The writing was in the King's hand, and he had left her a good amount of space for her illumination, about a third of the width of the parchment.

She began to read.

"What are you doing?" Wolsey's shout made her jerk.

She stared at him. "Reading the first paragraph."

His eyes widened, surprised, no doubt, that she *could* read. "For what reason?"

Susanna frowned. "So I have a sense of the contents. The painting needs to reflect the document."

"It is merely a congratulatory letter to the Emperor Charles on his victory over the French king. That is all you need to know."

Susanna met his gaze and then dipped her head. "As you wish, Your Grace." Her hand smoothed the parchment, trembling a little. She was to illuminate a missive for the Holy Roman Emperor. The man who ruled most of Europe.

She focused on the parchment, blocking out the space the King had left for the first letter of the missive, the *D* in *Deus*, and planning a short border that ran across the top and a little way down both sides of the document.

She loved the scratch of the charcoal on the parchment as she designed the border decoration—Tudor roses and the pomegranate of Katherine of Aragon on twisting, climbing vines, intertwined with birds, hunting hounds, and a cat whose paw she placed between the lines of writing, as if it were about to walk across the page.

Then she went to work on the *D* and the image she'd decided to include inside the letter—a miniature portrait of the King himself. She had drawn him twice before, and her charcoal moved with sure, swift strokes.

When she had done the rough sketches, she looked longingly at the gold leaf, but there wasn't time to mix the gesso.

Instead she would have to use powdered gold mixed with gum arabic, and that would wait until last.

She heard the door open, heard a murmured exchange, and vaguely registered that someone had placed a cup and a jug on the windowsill for her.

She carefully began inking the portrait, adding the first color, purple, for Henry's doublet. She frowned when she realized she couldn't see as well now, lifted her head, and blinked. The sun was setting and she could see herself reflected in the fine, expensive glass of the window. She rubbed her eyes and arched her back, lifting her shoulders and wincing at their stiffness.

A small movement caught her eye, and she turned to find Wolsey staring at her. The back of her neck pricked, and she found herself hunching over, as if to force his gaze away from her breasts.

"I need more light." Her voice was rough, her throat parched, and she reached for the watered wine that had been left for her.

Wolsey cleared his throat as she sipped and looked down at his papers. "There are candles in that cupboard over there."

She rose, wanting to stretch, to lift her arms above her head, but the hot, dark look in Wolsey's eyes when she had caught him staring made that impossible.

She pulled a tapestry across the window. Despite the glass, cold seeped into the room, and she felt instantly warmer as she twitched it into place.

She lined the desk with as many candles as practical.

Had Parker come? She had not heard him outside the door, but it was comforting to know Simon and Peter Jack were just beyond in the antechamber. And that Wolsey knew that, too.

Despite the lust she had seen on his face, he surely wouldn't try anything when a single cry from her would bring in two protectors.

She looked across at him, but his head was bent to his work and he did not look up. The tension in her neck and shoulders eased a little.

She worked on the head and shoulders portrait of Henry, then moved on to the D, until she had only the border left to do. She mixed her pigments, working her small stock of lapis lazuli with white until she had a sky blue. The color of loyalty, of dependability. However fast Wolsey wanted this done, she would put every nuance of her work to the King's advantage.

The birds, hounds, and cat looked beautiful against the blue; she had used bright jewel colors, and she wanted to scoop them up and let them chase and leap across her palm.

She finished with pen work in powdered gold, adding it first to the miniature portrait to create gold embroidery on Henry's shirt and doublet.

She had plenty of gold left, since she was planning to use it for the border, but she suddenly decided, extravagantly, to also use it in the letter D. To thread the whole letter with gold. It would frame the head and shoulders of the King beautifully.

She picked up her pen and began on the intricacies of her design. The Italian flourishes and curves, the tiny bracelet of cameos around the middle of the stem and the outer curve of the D, one of the King, the other of the Queen. It was so finely rendered, she doubted many would notice it, but it gave her pleasure to know it was there.

No doubt Wolsey would consider the time she had spent on it to be time wasted.

At last she moved to the border, and traced the Tudor roses and the pomegranates of the Queen in gold as well. Finally, she added a tiny gold bell around the cat's neck, to warn the birds of its approach.

Finished, she leaned back, closing her eyes and rolling her shoulders. Then she stood and, without looking at Wolsey, walked to the door and back.

She looked down at her work and thought it was good, and, given the time she had had, no ill reflection on her or her father's atelier.

"It is done?" Wolsey sat in shadow, and she wondered how long ago he had put his papers aside and begun watching her. When he had let his candle go out.

She nodded, sorry the King would never see this letter before it was sent. He was always a most appreciative patron, and he seemed to enjoy discussing her techniques with her.

Wolsey stood and crossed over to her.

She took a step back to give him better light, but also to put some distance between them.

Wolsey stared down, and when he turned to her his mouth was as severe as ever. She wondered, suddenly, if it was not the wait to have the document illuminated that so enraged him, but rather the document itself.

"When will it be dry enough to roll and seal?"

"If you leave it in a warm room, it will be dry by morning."

He gritted his teeth. "Very well. You may leave."

Susanna moved forward and began to pack her things away. Wolsey stood too close and she took less care than she would usually have done, hastily shoving everything back into her satchel.

He lifted a hand and for a moment she thought he was going to strike her, and she jerked back.

He stood, fingers extended, as if to brush her cheek, but his eyes were anything but tender. "Whatever you read while you worked on that document, I trust you will take care not to repeat."

Susanna nodded, a tight, sharp movement, and lifted her satchel. "Good evening, Your Grace."

He ignored her farewell. "That document was written by the King in his own hand, and read only by me. If you talk, I will know." He seemed to gather himself, as if to leap at her, a monster from a medieval illumination with crimson cloak swirling.

There was a sharp knock at the door, and Susanna felt her knees give a little in relief. Parker?

Wolsey kept watching her, not turning to the door as he called in answer, "Be gone."

Susanna put her arm behind her and flicked it; felt the new knife Parker had given her slip securely into her palm.

The door swung open, and Wolsey spun in rage. "I said, be gone, Simon Carter."

"Who is Simon Carter?" The man who stood in the door was a nobleman, in a rich velvet doublet. Susanna watched Wolsey's demeanor change in a blink, from fury to cold disdain.

She moved closer to the wall, skirting it on a path to the door, grateful her satchel had already been over her shoulder. Wolsey flicked a look in her direction, but he could do nothing to stop her.

The nobleman blocked the doorway and he gazed at her in open interest, taking in the smell of paint and the stains on her fingers as they clutched the satchel's straps.

"Who are you?"

"Susanna Horenbout, my lord, the King's painter."

"Ah, yes." He swung his gaze to the missive on the desk. "Are you making pretty the scurrilous writs of this bare-faced thief?"

Susanna's mouth gaped. "No, sir. A missive from the King."

Wolsey fixed his gaze on her, and she felt if he hadn't been sure the nobleman would have come to her rescue, his hands would have been around her throat for mentioning even that.

"Well, that is at least something. What he sent out last week was hard enough to swallow, without gold leaf."

"Go." Wolsey's eyes snapped at her, his voice harsh, and Susanna tried to inch past her rescuer.

He stepped forward, into the room, and Susanna saw his beefy fist close around Wolsey's robe at the neck. "This so-called Amicable Grant is illegal, Wolsey, plain and simple.

If you're trying to start civil unrest, you're doing a good job—because no one can pay what you're asking, sir. No one."

She stepped out of the room and slowly swung the doors shut.

"My tenants in Suffolk are on the verge of revolt." The nobleman's voice rose to a shout, but when the thick doors closed, the sound became too muffled to make out clearly.

Susanna turned and stopped short.

The antechamber was empty.

# 7

*War is not to be avoided, but is only to be put off to the advantage of others;*

—Machiavelli, The Prince, *chapter 3*

Susanna glanced behind her with a little spike of fear. She didn't want Wolsey to know she was alone and unprotected. Had he seen the room was empty as she'd stepped out?

She switched her knife to her other hand and swiped a fear-slicked palm down her wool dress.

Where were Simon and Peter Jack? Even if they were in the eating hall, she was surprised they would *both* leave.

She would find them.

She stepped out of the antechamber, closing the door quietly behind her, and a hand tapped her shoulder from behind. She spun on her heel with a strangled shriek.

It was a man in the Cardinal's livery. She put one hand to

her heart, half-raised the other, knife still clutched between stiff fingers, and stared at him, breathing fast.

"My pardon, mistress. Does His Grace require anything?" He either didn't see her weapon in the gloom or chose to ignore it.

She shook her head.

"My thanks." The man shuffled back to a chair set in a dark alcove of the passageway.

Able at last to draw a breath, Susanna wondered if he realized how close he'd come to having his throat cut. She readjusted her grip on her knife. "Did you see which way my companions went?"

"I've seen no one."

Susanna could feel the Cardinal's presence and wanted, needed, to flee. She turned in the direction she'd come, trying to remember the twists and turns Simon had taken to deliver her into the Cardinal's lair.

With the King gone to stay in one of his country houses to hawk, Bridewell was eerily empty. Some of the passageways had not been lit, and Susanna walked with a hand against the wall, swinging out to avoid chairs and hall tables.

The smell of beeswax, lemon, and vinegar was strong. Evidence the servants had been hard at work while they had the chance to clean thoroughly.

At last, up ahead she saw lights, and realized she was all but running toward them. She forced herself to slow, to breathe deep, and stepped out into a main hall.

She recognized it, and recalled the way out into the courtyard.

There was no sign of Simon or Peter Jack, and she began to worry. They would never have left her alone willingly, even without the threat of Parker's anger hanging over them.

A few servants looked in her direction. They were gathered around a small fireplace at the far end of the hall and although it made sense to approach them, Susanna suddenly felt very foreign, very out of place.

She was exposed, too. If the Cardinal came looking for her he would see her, no matter which passageway he used. She moved closer to the door to the backyard and tucked herself behind a heavy support beam.

After some minutes had passed, she peered around. The Cardinal's man had joined the servants at the fire, and one suddenly pointed in her direction.

Heart thumping, Susanna looked at the door that led to the stables. Wolsey's man began walking toward her, and she considered her chances of finding help here against the man who ruled England for the King.

She ran for the door.

———

A bitter March wind had started up and Susanna pulled her cloak about herself as she headed for the stables, hurrying within before Wolsey's man could see her direction. She shuddered with relief as she stepped into the warm, ripe air of the barn, and her cheeks burned with the change in temperature.

"Aye?" The groomsman who stepped forward eyed her suspiciously.

"I'm looking for Simon Carter." She was fascinated by his face, by the deep wrinkles at his eyes, the dimple in his cheek.

The man relaxed. "You'd be Parker's lady, eh?"

She nodded. "I can't find Simon to take me home."

The man scratched his head. "I haven't seen him. His cart's still here." He pointed and Susanna recognized Simon's cart, and his two horses feeding quietly beside it.

Simon might have been called to other duties, but Peter Jack's disappearance was inexplicable. She turned back to the door out to the yard, torn between worry for him and fear of the Cardinal. Rain began drumming on the stable roof.

"Why aren't you waiting inside—begging your pardon at the question—mistress?"

Susanna turned to the groomsman, unsure whether to answer truthfully. Wolsey was not the master of Bridewell, but all knew he acted for the King. "I'm afraid of someone within." It was the most truthful thing she could say.

"Someone behaving ill?" The man rubbed his cheek. "Does he know you're Parker's lady, and all?"

Susanna lifted her shoulders.

He pursed his lips. "Most likely not. You can stay here, then. Simon won't go anywhere without his cart and his animals." He gave a small bow. "Name's Alfred, mistress."

Susanna curtsied back. "I am Susanna Horenbout."

After the intricate, delicate work of the illumination, she felt like a bolder, larger challenge. And she loved the good humor on his face. "Would you let me sketch your portrait?"

# 8

*And although they were great and wonderful men, yet they were men, and each one of them had no more opportunity than the present offers, for their enterprises were neither more just nor easier than this, nor was God more their friend than He is yours.*

—Machiavelli, The Prince, *chapter 26*

Parker's frustration and anger were like a sack of rocks, bumping and bruising him with each step. He'd lost the assassin south of the river—a thick fog and increased foot traffic conspiring to rob him of a chance to run his quarry to ground.

Unless he'd been deliberately led on and dropped. Parker didn't want to contemplate that possibility. It would mean he'd wasted the whole afternoon and had no starting point at which to try to pick up his man again.

He walked into his courtyard and frowned. The only light in the house came from the kitchen.

There was no sound from the barn, but Parker stuck his head around the door anyway. The horses looked up curiously from their feed, and then went back to their supper.

Parker closed the door, and as he stepped out from the eaves the rain came, suddenly, in a soft hiss of sound.

The thought of Susanna waiting within, in the warmth, made him run through the puddles to the back door with a lighter step.

He stepped in and the wind wrenched the door from his hand and slammed it against the wall.

As he struggled to close it, he registered Mistress Greene and Eric, their eyes wide with the shock of the slamming door and the suddenness of his entrance.

They were sitting beside the fire, in a way that reminded him of a vigil. Mistress Greene stood and suddenly an icy knife twisted in his gut.

"Susanna?"

"Not here." Mistress Greene wound the corner of her apron around her hand. "The King ordered her to Bridewell Palace."

"The King?" Parker frowned.

"Aye, to paint some important document for him. Simon came to fetch her."

Parker relaxed a little. "Peter Jack went, too?"

They nodded in unison.

Parker turned back to the door, hand extended to open it again. It swung inward of its own accord.

Peter Jack stood dripping outside. His eyes lifted and the look in them shot a bolt of pure terror into Parker's heart.

There was a gray-green tinge to Peter Jack's skin, and he had clearly stumbled and fallen a number of times on his way home.

"I ate something . . ." He pushed a muddy hand through his hair. "I've been sick all afternoon, and when I got to the Cardinal's rooms she wasn't there. Simon had already told me we'd have to find our own way home, so I know she hasn't gone with him."

Parker stepped back so Peter Jack could come into the warm kitchen, but he would not move.

"I've lost her, sir. She's gone."

---

Parker came for her, striding out of the darkness like Hades in search of his bride.

Susanna watched him, fascinated, from her perch on a hay bale. She'd just finished a detailed charcoal of Simon's horses, but here was something infinitely more interesting to draw.

He'd pushed the stable doors open, striking them with open palms, and stopped short at the sight of her, his mouth grim and his eyes filled with the curious blankness they assumed when he was prepared to do infinite harm, commit any violence.

Her heart almost stopped beating at the power and danger of him, and at the way his face softened in the three steps it took him to reach her and draw her into his arms.

He did not speak, and neither did she. The only sound was the drip of water as it fell in a steady stream from Parker's cloak onto the stone floor of the stable.

There was a scrape of a boot behind them and Parker tensed. Susanna put out a hand to still him.

"We kept 'er safe, sir." Alfred shuffled forward and Parker stepped back a little, his arm still around her.

"I thank you for it." Parker gave a half bow.

Susanna began packing away her things. "This is for you, Alfred." She held out a second sketch she had made of him, forking hay.

He took it and gaped as he held it to the light. "Aye, and I can see why the King called you from over the sea, mistress. It's as if you trapped me on paper. Aren't I the lucky one, getting sommat same as the King?"

"Thank you for letting me stay here." She lifted her satchel.

Parker took it from her hands. "Peter Jack is looking for you, too. We have to find him."

"I'm glad he's safe. I was worried about him." She let Parker draw her toward the door and gave a final wave to Alfred before stepping out under the eaves to watch the rain fall in rhythmic sheets.

Parker closed the stable doors behind them and turned to her, his face shuttered. "You took years off my life, my lady. I am aged."

Susanna smiled and looked up into his eyes, as blue as the border she'd used in the King's document. "I knew you would come to find me. And I did not want to walk back alone in the rain and dark."

"No." He raised a brow. "That would have been even worse."

"I thought I would have to, but Alfred hid me when he came looking in the stable—"

"Who came looking?"

Susanna shivered, like a cat, from the top of her spine down. "The Cardinal's man."

She saw him frown, confused.

"The Cardinal wishes me ill."

He stared at her.

"Did he touch you?" His words were calm, but his eyes made her think of a blizzard.

"He tried, after I finished the illumination. A nobleman came in just at that moment to argue about some grant the Cardinal has ordered people to pay. I managed to get out, but his man came looking for me. When I couldn't find Simon or Peter Jack, I chose to wait in the stables, near Simon's cart."

"You did well." He looked at her steadily. "No matter the situation, you always do well."

The smile she gave him came from deep within, and she blinked to hold back the tears that suddenly threatened to fall.

"Which nobleman interrupted Wolsey?"

She cleared her throat. "I don't know. I wish I did. I want to paint his portrait, or his wife's, as a thank-you. He saved me from having to stab the Cardinal." She laughed, weakly. "The knife was ready, in my hand. And then, no doubt, I would have had to flee back to Ghent."

"Did someone enter the Cardinal's office while you were working?"

She cocked her head in thought; shrugged. "I have no notion. Wait—yes, someone did come in, but I was too busy to look up. Why?"

"The Cardinal instructed them to give Peter Jack some refreshment." He frowned. "Peter Jack spent the afternoon in the garderobe, with his head in the gong."

"They poisoned him?" Rage flashed through her, hot and wild.

"So it seems. When he told me, I thought it was bad food from the kitchen, but not now."

"And yet he came back with you?" She looked at him, aghast.

"Nothing could have stopped him returning."

"Then let's find him."

He held his hand out to her and she took it, remembering a time not so long ago when he had done the same thing, almost in this same spot. The rain had been falling just as hard then, too.

As they ran across the courtyard, rain soaking through her cloak, she reflected that they were in as much trouble now as they had been then.

She had trusted him last time, with no idea if that was wise. Now she knew it was the best decision she had ever made.

# 9

*For among other evils which being unarmed brings you, it causes you to be despised, and this is one of those ig-nominies against which a prince ought to guard himself.*

—Machiavelli, The Prince, *chapter 14*

"Maggie says he'll live." Susanna sank into her chair by the fire and rubbed her arms.

"I told you that already." Parker did not open his eyes.

She turned her head. "He looked green. I've never seen him so weak. Or so upset."

Parker shrugged. "There is no help for that. He lost you and he feels the failure of it."

"Talk to him." She reached out and took his hand. "Please. He was bested by no less an enemy than the man who runs England."

Parker still kept his eyes shut. "You have it right. I will talk to him. It wasn't his fault."

"I wonder . . ." She hesitated a moment, staring at the fire, not wanting to talk of Wolsey and stoke Parker's anger again. She lifted her head and was caught in his gaze. He'd gone from sprawled in his chair to quiet readiness for action in a moment.

"You wonder what?"

"If Wolsey was going to . . . attack me because of the missive."

"Why would he do that?"

"To intimidate me. Make sure I told no one what the King was proposing to the Emperor."

"And what was he proposing?" She had his full attention.

"He proposes raising an English army to take all of France, while Charles holds the King of France hostage." Her fingers were still entwined in his, and she tugged them free. "It was written in the King's own hand. No one has read that letter but Wolsey and myself."

"It is rumored in court Wolsey has the pox. And he did not get that without bedding his share of women." Parker tapped his fist deliberately against the arm of his chair. "Perhaps he wanted you; perhaps he wanted to force you into silence; perhaps both."

She worried her bottom lip. "He is afraid of that letter. He doesn't like what it says and he doesn't want anyone else to know what's in it."

Parker shook his head. "That's because he hopes the King of France will put him forward as a candidate for pope. The Emperor promised twice to advance him, and broke his word both times. Wolsey has lost all trust in him. His only chance now is through France."

"But the King of France is a prisoner."

"Francis will be released. The Emperor will reach some arrangement with him; he won't hold on to the King of France forever. And Wolsey knows we cannot successfully conquer France. We don't have the money. If we try and fail—and we *will* fail—especially while Francis is hostage, he will not look kindly on England when he is set free. Wolsey will forever lose his chance to be pope."

"Why would the French king help Wolsey, though? Why would he advance Wolsey before anyone else?" Susanna leaned her head back against the chair.

"Wolsey might have promised to steer Henry away from a war with France." Parker shrugged. "It would be an empty offer, though. Henry relies on Wolsey but he is not afraid to act of his own accord. Francis knows it, too. If there is a promise between them, it must be something else."

"Something that would be compromised by that letter. Wolsey's hands were shaking. He didn't want to hand it to me to illuminate."

Parker stroked his thumb across his chin. "It would be useful to find out."

There was a sound of voices and then the heavy tread of a man's footsteps coming down the passage from the kitchen.

Parker stood, fluid and fast, and picked up his sword from the table. His knife was in his hand and his eyes on the door. "Curl up in the chair, make yourself small."

Susanna lifted her feet and hugged her knees, tucking her gown about her so she was invisible from the doorway.

Parker moved toward the door, and she heard him fling it open.

"Simon." He spoke as if he had not been prepared to kill.

Susanna got to her feet and looked over the top of her chair. She saw Simon's eyes on Parker's knife and sword, still held casually in reach of Simon's throat.

"I'm sorry about Susanna. Alfred told me there was some trouble, but I had no choice."

Parker raised a brow.

"The King was nearly killed." Simon's voice rose. "He fell into a ditch while hawking. His pole snapped as he was vaulting over it. He was stuck, headfirst, in the mud. A groom saved his life."

"Is he well?"

"Aye." Simon rubbed a hand through his hair. "It seems he's well enough, but his doctor wants all manner of medicines brought out to the country. I've been running helter skelter all afternoon trying to lay hands on what he's ordered me to bring up."

"This will stir up the worries about succession again." Parker put his knife away but held on to his sword.

"It's already started. The King is not unaware of it, either. He's coming back to London as soon as possible." Simon stepped into the room at last, catching Susanna's eye and bowing. "I am sorry for leaving you, but with Peter Jack there—"

"Peter Jack was poisoned." Her throat felt hot.

Simon gaped. "By whom?"

"Who is the Cardinal's man? The one who sits outside his rooms?" Parker ran his thumb over the hilt of his sword.

"I don't know." Simon looked between them, and Susanna saw him swallow hard as the implication of the question sank in.

Parker lifted his sword and slid it into its scabbard with an audible snick in the silence. "Then we'll find out."

# 10

*I conclude, therefore that, fortune being changeful and
mankind steadfast in their ways, so long as the two are
in agreement men are successful, but unsuccessful when
they fall out.*

—Machiavelli, The Prince, *chapter 25*

"If you need to vomit while I'm talking to Gittens, aim at
him, not me." Parker put a hand out to steady Peter
Jack, and waited for him to catch his breath just within the
great hall of Bridewell Palace.

Peter Jack drew a shuddering gulp of air into his lungs and
stood taller. "I'm well enough."

"You should be in bed."

Peter Jack shot him a look that made Parker grin. Maybe
the lad *was* well enough. Parker wouldn't have stayed in bed,
either, had he been poisoned and then offered a chance to
speak face-to-face with the poisoner.

He led on and Peter Jack followed, his breathing a little
too quick and shallow.

A murmur of voices came from the eating hall behind the great room. Only the servants of administrators who had not accompanied the King, and those who stayed behind to clean were there. Parker stood quietly in the doorway, searching for his prey before anyone noticed him.

"There." Peter Jack pointed to the man Parker had discovered was Isaac Gittens. He was sitting with two others, holding a piece of bread in one hand and a mug of ale in another. His face was lined and his back stooped a little, but Gittens was not frail.

Parker closed in.

One by one, the conversations stopped as he passed the long tables, until the only ones talking were Gittens and his two friends.

One of the men looked up, confused by the silence, and his gaze met Parker's. His eyes widened.

"What is . . ." Gittens turned on the bench and froze with the hunk of bread halfway to his mouth.

"Good day, Gittens. A word in private?"

Gittens had the sense to shake his head. "I'll go nowhere with you." He flicked his gaze behind Parker to Peter Jack, and dropped his bread.

Parker leaned forward and Gittens's left eye twitched. "I'll give you a choice." He kept his voice reasonable. "You'll stand up and walk out with me for a private talk, or I'll drag you out with a knife to your throat."

"Not in front of the whole hall, you wouldn't." Gittens lifted his mug of ale to his lips, and Parker watched the thoughts chase across his eyes. As Gittens set his mouth on the lip of the mug and lifted it up, Parker stepped to the side and forward, up close. His hand came down hard on Gittens's back the moment after the Cardinal's man spat his drink at where Parker had been.

He choked convulsively, and Parker lifted him up by the collar of his doublet. "Wouldn't I?"

He tightened his grip and flicked a quick look at Gittens's friends. They had not moved.

"Let's go." He dragged Gittens, still coughing, to the back of the hall and into a narrow passage that led out to the kitchen gardens.

Peter Jack followed behind him, brushing droplets of ale from his sleeves.

By the time they reached the outside door, Gittens had stopped choking. He tried to twist away, made himself a dead-weight.

Parker threw him headfirst into the garden.

Gittens landed well, rolling to the side and trying to scrabble to his feet, but Parker had his sword out and just short of his eye while he was still on his knees.

"I'm the Cardinal's man." Gittens licked his lips, nervous little flicks of his tongue like a lizard's.

"Aye. It makes it all the more interesting, doesn't it?" Parker moved his blade lightly down the side of Gittens's cheek.

Gittens shivered but held firm. "He won't take this well."

"I think whatever Wolsey feels about this personally, he

will not go complaining to the King about me. Or no more than he usually does." Parker smiled. "Because he has tried to get rid of me so many times now, the King simply ignores him. Like the little boy who cried wolf."

Gittens shrank back. "What do you want?"

"You caused harm to my page so your master could molest my betrothed. That's two wrongs you've committed against me, Gittens. Two serious wrongs."

Gittens shifted his gaze to Peter Jack, then back to Parker. "I didn't know she was your betrothed." He swallowed, his Adam's apple bobbing in his throat. "She didn't come to any harm—"

"No thanks to you. And certainly no thanks to your master."

Gittens shivered again, through his whole body. "The Cardinal is not himself."

"What's he hatching?" Parker lifted his blade back to Gittens's eye.

Gittens held very still. "He don't tell the likes of me." His voice was rough, bitter. "Plays everything very close. Always has. But it's to do with that Frenchie, I'm guessing."

Parker held his face blank. "Frenchie?"

Gittens looked despairingly at the blade at eye level. "Never seen his face. Hardly seen *him*. He slips in and out like a shadow." He leaned back from the tip of Parker's sword a little and raised his eyes. "Wouldn't want to meet him in a dark alley."

"Is that so?" Parker lifted his blade and Gittens flinched

back. He sheathed it and stepped away, gestured to Peter Jack. "All yours."

Gittens's face was bleak. "I didn't think the dose'd affect you that bad. Forgot you weren't full-grown."

Peter Jack looked at Gittens, his eyes going over the mud splashed on his shirt and covering his legs, flecks of it drying on his cheeks and forehead. "When I *am* full-grown, don't ever turn your back on me."

He spun on his heel and walked away, leaving Gittens gaping after him.

The lad had been watching and listening. Parker would give him that.

# 11

*The wish to acquire is in truth very natural and
common, and men always do so when they can, and for
this they will be praised not blamed; but when they
cannot do so, yet wish to do so by any means, then
there is folly and blame.*

—Machiavelli, The Prince, *chapter 3*

Parker heard the murmurs and mutterings of complaint
before he reached Wolsey's antechamber.

He stepped into the room and found it crowded with
well-dressed merchants and noblemen. A contingent of some
kind.

"Parker, you here to join us?" Edward Malory, a landholder
from near Parker's own country estates, elbowed through the
crowd and stood before him.

Parker shook his head. "What is this about?"

Malory cast a poisoned look at Wolsey's door. "That crimi-
nal has bypassed Parliament and issued a writ to levy a grant
from the clergy and the laity. Calls it the Amicable Grant."

"On whose authority?"

Malory looked suddenly uncomfortable. "We hope his own. If the King's behind it . . ."

Parker swung his gaze around the room. If the King was behind this, it would make it harder to fight. But if it was illegal, the King might well pretend to have nothing to do with it, even if he was the instigator.

"What does Wolsey say the money's for?"

"To raise an army to invade France." Malory gestured behind him. "All well and good, but on top of the other taxes, this is too much. There are going to be people dying of starvation if this goes through. We can't afford for the people to be so affected. The men who work in the town around my lands are agitated enough to cause some real damage, and I can't blame them."

"What do you plan to do?" Parker wondered if Wolsey had foreseen this kind of trouble.

"Fight him. In the courts if we have to. Through Parliament. Whatever it takes."

"Is he in there?" Parker jerked his head in the direction of Wolsey's door.

"We think so. We saw him come in here, but he won't come out."

Parker moved toward the door and gave a short, sharp rap against it.

There was silence. The men in the room had gone quiet, too.

Parker cupped a hand over his mouth. "It's Gittens, my lord. Message from the King."

He heard the thud of footsteps and a scrabble in the lock. The door swung open, and Parker ducked beneath Wolsey's arm.

As the men in the antechamber surged forward, Wolsey slammed the door shut and turned the key.

"Parker." Wolsey stared at him stony-faced, his lips as thin and mean as a stale crust of bread. His eyes were bloodshot, with dark circles under them. His face was sheened in sweat as though he had a fever, and he was the deathly white of a funeral shroud.

"You tried to molest my betrothed last night, Wolsey. Did you think I would let it go?"

Wolsey started. "Your betrothed? I had heard the King has given you leave to marry, but I did not realize—" He cut off. Rubbed his temple with a plump, ink-stained finger. "I remember hearing something, but I have been overwhelmed recently and did not comprehend . . ."

Parker said nothing, and the silence stretched out between them.

One of the men in the antechamber slammed a fist into the door, and Wolsey jumped at the sound.

He caught himself, seeming to realize what he looked like, hiding in his own chamber.

"Get out, Parker." Those thin lips twisted in a snarl and he lifted his arm dismissively. "There is nothing you can do to me, and the wench is fine, although why you would want a harridan like that—"

Parker pinned Wolsey to the door with a forearm under his neck.

Wolsey gave a shout of surprise, tried to pull himself free. He stopped as Parker's knife came up to his throat, and his eyes widened as the blade came to rest lightly against his skin.

"I want to kill you. It won't be easy to do, but if you try anything like that again, I will find a way." Parker tugged his other knife from his boot and stepped back, a blade in each hand.

Wolsey sagged against the door. "Be gone, Parker. I can hire a blade to run you through far easier than you would be able to kill me without repercussions."

"You mean your French assassin?" Parker thought Wolsey's knees gave a little more. He put his knives away. "I wouldn't count on him anymore."

"What?" The question came out in a croak. Wolsey stepped away from the door and used the wall to keep himself steady.

Parker dipped his head in farewell, turned the key, and threw the door open. "Gentlemen, he's all yours."

---

Harry was looking more dangerous every time Susanna saw him. It disturbed her, made her chest tighten.

His hair had been a dark, matted mess when she'd first met him, his face dirty and his clothes rags. Now that Parker was paying him, and providing him and his little gang of lads with lodgings a few streets away, he didn't look like a feral urchin anymore.

His hair was clean and a beautiful golden brown. His clothes were warm and serviceable, just the right quality and cut for an apprentice or a merchant's aide. He was filling those clothes out better, too. They no longer hung on him like a scarecrow's wardrobe.

She'd invited him into the study when he'd arrived at the back door, and he was watching her now with eyes as keen and sharp as they'd ever been.

Eyes like Peter Jack and Eric. Eyes like old men.

"Parker could find you a real apprenticeship, Harry." Susanna sat and gestured to Parker's chair.

"The arrangement I have with him seems very real to me." Harry sat stiff and straight, not the slightest bend in his back.

"It *is* so real, you must surely be the image of him at the same age, hair and eye color aside."

Harry seemed very pleased by that. Too pleased.

"Parker went down the road he did because he had no choice, Harry. He had no benefactor as you do now. He had no one to give him a chance at advancement."

Harry stared back at her. "Don't you like what Parker is?"

"Like?" She laughed. "I love Parker exactly as he is. But he lived a hard, cold life, and a lonely one. I want to protect you from that if I can."

Harry thought about it for a moment. "And Peter Jack and Eric?"

"Peter Jack is often at Parker's side; he's learning the respectable end of Parker's business. It worries me you are learning . . ." She sighed. She did not know how to proceed without causing offense.

"The darker side?" Harry smiled.

It reminded her so much of Parker, it hurt. She nodded.

"The darker side suits me better." Harry lifted his hands with a shrug, leaned back a little in the chair, and allowed it to take his weight.

Susanna clenched her hands into fists in her lap, but there was nothing else to say on the matter. "You came to report to Parker?"

"Aye." Harry was watching her again, as if weighing up whether to tell her the news instead of Parker. "An urchin dropped a note at the Duke's this morning. Norfolk came flying out of the house when he got it, but by then the urchin had gone."

"You followed the lad?"

Harry nodded. "He had just nipped around the corner for the rest of his money. Foreign man gave it to him. I thought you might like to know that when he spoke to the lad, his words sounded like yours."

Susanna started. "You mean he spoke English like I do? Like a person from the Lowlands?"

"It is a most pleasant accent, and I recognized it immediately."

Susanna blew out a breath. This should not surprise her. Jens had been involved, after all. Why not more of her countrymen? "Did you follow the man after he paid the lad?"

Harry raised a brow at her and despite herself, she laughed. "Of course you did."

"He walked back to one those narrow houses set on London Bridge." Harry looked suddenly uneasy.

"What?"

"They seem to be packing up and leaving."

"Right now?" Parker was at Bridewell. It would take at least an hour to fetch him back.

"They are heaping their things into a cart at the door."

"Perhaps I can slow them down, if they are from the Low Countries. Pretend some connection to them?"

Harry's fingers gripped and released the wool of his breeches. "Parker will not like it." But the excitement of the chase was in his eyes.

Susanna stood. "Parker does not like a lot of things. But he will dislike losing this man even more." And she would go out of her way to foil any plan of Norfolk's.

"You can take me to London Bridge. I'll send Eric to wait for Parker and Peter Jack outside Bridewell, to tell them where we are."

Harry nodded and rose, too.

"You hoped I'd suggest this, didn't you?" Susanna watched him form a denial, then nod, a tiny movement of his head.

The thrill of the chase. The determination to bring down the prey. Maybe it was living on the streets, as Parker had—although Peter Jack had done that, too, and he didn't have the same wild edge as Harry.

Whatever the reason, Susanna was glad Parker had found Harry and taken him in.

He was already a strong adversary, and when he grew into the promise of his height and his hands, he would be almost as dangerous as her lover.

And loyal only to him.

# 12

*Those who strive to obtain the good graces of a prince
are accustomed to come before him with such things as
they hold most precious, or in which they see him take
most delight; whence one often sees horses, arms, cloth
of gold, precious stones, and similar ornaments presented to princes, worthy of their greatness.*

—Machiavelli, The Prince, *dedication*

Parker had sent Peter Jack back to Crooked Lane, but now
he regretted it.

The occupants of the house Pettigrew had visited on
London Bridge were packing up, and Parker would've felt happier to have Peter Jack or Harry with him, to follow if the cart
went one way and the man Pettigrew had spoken to another.

He'd wanted to take some control, instead of being flotsam
on a raging tide, and his decision to come here, rather than
wander the streets where he'd lost the assassin the afternoon
before, had served him well.

The pile of furniture and trunks being loaded into the cart
was growing. If he'd come half an hour later, he might have
missed them.

He watched the house from a sheltered corner of a stall selling pies. The pie seller had urged him to stand awhile out of the wind, and it was a good place to loiter.

He lifted the meat pie to his mouth and took a bite, and rich flavor, lamb cooked with wine and rosemary, spilled onto his tongue.

"I will be back to buy more," he said, his mouth half full, and the stallholder grinned.

"This is a good spot for you," Parker commented casually as the man wrapped up six pies for another customer. He pointed to the houses on the north side of the bridge. "Those who live nearby buy from you often, I have no doubt."

The stallholder snorted. "Some do. Some don't."

"Who would not?" He kept his tone mildly curious.

"The Englishmen do, that's true." The pie seller tied the bundle of pies with string. "The foreigners, though, they ain't used to our cooking."

"There are a lot of foreigners living on the bridge?" Parker watched heat flare in the seller's eyes.

"One's more than there should be, you ask me. I've been trying to rent rooms in a house here for years. *Years*. If I could live nearer my stall, or have a little shop instead of a stall, it would be much easier—but the rents they want." He shook his head. "Then some wealthy foreigners come and move in."

"And don't buy your pies, on top of it." Parker's voice was dry.

The stallholder nodded. "Aye. Insult to injury."

"But I'm curious; where do these foreigners come from?"

"The ones across there, the ones leaving." The stallholder pointed at the cart. "From the Low Countries."

"Ah." Parker swallowed the last of his pie. "Merchants?"

The stallholder shrugged. "Cloth. Some say 'tis very fine."

Parker let his gaze wander to the house again. "Well, perhaps a few rooms in the house will be available to you, as they seem to be taking everything with them."

The pie seller twisted his mouth in an expression that said he wouldn't hold his breath.

Parker turned away and began to walk slowly past the other stalls, allowing himself to be jostled by the traffic, his eyes never leaving the cart.

What had Norfolk wanted from here, that he had sent Pettigrew to get for him? And what had put the fright into his informer?

He tensed as a couple approached the cart, skirted around it, and stepped up to the door.

The man guarding the cart called out to them and the woman turned to respond, lifting the hood of her cloak and speaking in a foreign tongue.

Parker's mouth dropped open, and he closed it with a snap.

It was Susanna.

———

"WHo are you?" The man beside the cart switched to Flemish.

"Susanna Horenbout, of Ghent, sir. I heard a friend of my father's might be living here, and I came to inquire."

The man's fists uncurled, but when he looked at Harry, his eyes were hard.

"And him?" He jerked his head in Harry's direction.

"My page. It is very dangerous in this city, no? Not like Ghent."

"True enough." He looked around him sourly. "Not that I'm from Ghent, but anywhere in the Low Countries would show well next to this cesspit."

"I see that you are leaving. Are you going back home?"

He nodded, curt and suddenly silent.

Susanna felt Harry fidget beside her. She wasn't moving fast enough for him. "Could you tell me who lives here? I am not sure I have come to the right place." She smiled at the cart man as if they shared a secret. "My father does not understand how large London is, and he has a friend living somewhere near here. I heard a fellow countryman was in this house, and thought perhaps it was the man my father is urging me to visit."

The man shifted, wary, but before he could answer her the door opened, and two men wrestled a heavy chest down the steps.

Harry drew in a surprised breath, and she could feel his body tense.

"That is the last one." One of the men stood back, brushing his doublet and breathing deeply. He was better dressed than the other two, and his hair and hands looked well tended.

He gave a startled shout when he caught sight of Susanna and tried to cover it, placing a hand to his heart.

"My apologies, my lady. I did not realize I had visitors."

"I am sorry to startle you." Susanna curtsied deeply. "I am from Ghent and—"

"A fellow countrywoman." He laughed, the sound too wild, too full of relief. "As you see, we are on our way home, and very busy."

"I apologize for disturbing you, sir. Had I known you were leaving, I would of course have come sooner, but I was told someone in this house was perhaps a friend of my father, and that I should visit you—"

"Someone mentioned me by name?" He spoke as if there were hands around his throat, squeezing.

"No. Someone at court—"

"Who?" He reached out, grabbing her arm in a tight grip, but even as Harry stepped forward a hand shot out from the street, squeezing the man's arm so hard, Susanna saw his face go pale.

Parker.

The man slid his gaze left. "Unhand me, sir." He spoke in Flemish, but his meaning was clear.

"Not until you unhand my lady."

Susanna winced. Parker was speaking through gritted teeth.

"What's this?" The cart man took a step toward them, but Parker's gaze did not leave her assailant's face.

Harry's hand slid to his boot.

There was a pause, the threat of violence hanging clear in the air, then the grip on her arm was suddenly gone. She took a step back, rubbing the spot. There would be a bruise. Something for Parker to grumble about later, she was sure.

"That was swift indeed, my lord." She couldn't keep the surprise from her voice. "I sent Eric to find you not twenty minutes ago."

"Did you? I must have missed him." He spoke as if his jaws were locked together, and suddenly Susanna wanted to laugh. She realized if they were alone, he would quite cheerfully be strangling her.

"Who do you seek, my lady?" The gentleman edged closer to his door.

Susanna lifted her gaze to his. "I seek one of my father's close friends. Jens of Antwerp."

The man stumbled on the steps, then he spun to the doorway and ran through it.

# 13

*For injuries ought to be done all at one time, so that,
being tasted less, they offend less; benefits ought to be
given little by little, so that the flavour of them may last
longer.*

—Machiavelli, The Prince, *chapter 8*

Parker watched the merchant run into his hole, a hole
with no escape. The door of the house stood open and he
hauled Susanna with him up the stairs and into the entrance
hall. Harry was right on his heels and as soon as he was in,
Parker slammed the door shut and locked it.

He ignored the shouts and hammering from the street.

He turned and eyed the two of them with annoyance.
"What are you doing here?"

"I followed the cart driver from Norfolk's to this house earlier." Harry avoided his stare. "He gave a note to a boy to deliver to the Duke, and stayed to make sure it was. Upset the
Duke mightily, it did."

"Mmmm."

"I saw they were packing up, came to find you, but you weren't home." Harry concentrated on pulling his knife from his boot.

Susanna put a hand on his arm. "I suggested sending Eric to get you. When Harry told me they were from the Low Countries, I thought I might be able to delay them." She smiled at him, serene and beautiful, as perplexing as a warm wind in winter. And as devastating.

"Why did you think to offer up Jens's name?" It was the most dangerous one she could have given, no matter that it had produced the most startling result.

"It was all I could think of."

"My lord." Harry at last looked up at him. "When the merchant came down the stairs with that chest I recognized him right away, but had no chance to tell Mistress Horenbout."

"Recognized him?" Parker frowned.

"Aye. He was the man who visited Jens for ten minutes the night he was killed."

Parker felt the first flames of success warming his belly. This was progress. "Let us go ask our man a few questions." He unsheathed his sword, flicked his knife into his hand. The merchant was desperate enough to be dangerous.

From a room at the back he heard shutters bang, and with a feeling of dread he raced down the hall and flung open the door to a good-sized room stripped almost bare. The shutters were hanging wide-open.

Could the merchant be so mad as to go into the water?

He reached the window and peered down, leaning over the

edge to see the man climbing down a rope ladder attached to hooks in the wall.

The ladder hung against the brick and stone of the bridge and swayed as the merchant grappled with it. Down below, a huddle of boats bided their time a short distance from the bridge, waiting for the waters to calm.

Parker could hear the roar that came with the ebb tide. The river was cut off by the bridge, choked suddenly in its journey and forced to squeeze itself between the narrow spans. There would be a difference in the level of water from one side of the bridge to the other of perhaps a man's height, and Parker could see its raging power, the churning white foam flinging up a fine spray.

He sheathed his sword, slipped his knife back up his sleeve, and swung himself out over the window.

"No!" Susanna's shout jerked his head up as he took the first step.

"I can't let him get away." Parker tested the strength of the rope and took another step down.

"What do you want me to do, sir?" Harry's head joined Susanna's.

"Take my lady and meet me down below on the bank."

"Parker." Susanna's eyes were wide, her voice faint, as if from lack of breath.

Before, he would have thrown himself into the chase with no fears, but he had so much more to lose these days.

He reached up and touched her hand, then moved down the rope as fast as he could. The wind whipped up by the raging water lifted his cloak about him, battering his face and getting in his eyes.

When he was halfway down, he risked a look between his feet and saw he was gaining on his quarry. What could he do when he caught the merchant that wouldn't endanger them both?

Now that he was lower down, nearer the river, he heard a faint sound of shouting over the roar of the water, and turned his head to see the watermen gesturing and calling.

Telling him and the merchant they were mad, no doubt, and he couldn't disagree. The merchant was nearly at the end of the rope ladder, and he dropped down onto the pier at the base of the pillar.

He began to call to the watermen, waving at them to collect him.

Parker moved faster. It would be madness for the watermen to sail under the bridge at ebb tide, but some of the watermen *were* mad. They shot the bridge as a badge of honor, braving the torrent and flying through the air to the other side.

The merchant looked up and for a moment they stared at each other, gazes locked.

With a wrench, the merchant looked away, scrabbling in an inner pocket. He drew out a gem and held it up to the light.

"A boat!" he screamed over the waterfall of sound. "This for a boat!"

One of the boats moved, the waterman letting the current

sweep him toward them. Before he was sucked into the narrow arch, he fought the water with his oars and spun the boat, so it came to rest against the pier.

Parker moved faster. Twice he missed his footing and found himself with feet dangling, his heart in his mouth.

With a cry, the merchant leaped into the boat. Parker stopped and saw the boat rock wildly under the onslaught.

The waterman held out his hand, and the merchant placed the gem in his palm.

With a flip of his oar, the waterman spun the boat back into the maelstrom, and the boat was sucked through the arch.

"To me! To me!" Parker dropped onto the pier, his throat raw as he shouted over the pounding noise. He lifted his money belt. "To me—King's business!"

At last a boat came forward, spinning twice before it reached the pier, hitting the stone with a crack of wood.

Parker dropped into the small vessel, pushing himself back as his feet touched the bottom to make his impact less.

"You landed better than t'other one." The waterman spat. "Money?"

"Aye." Parker dug into his purse and produced three sovereigns. "King's business. Follow them."

"Always wanted to work for the King." The waterman chuckled and pushed them away from the swells at the pillar with an oar.

For a moment they were in free spin, the water turning them as if they were in a whirlpool, and then, with a force that threw Parker's head back and sent his cloak streaming behind him, the current grabbed hold of them and shot them like a rock from a catapult through the arch.

Darkness and noise pressed against him from all sides, spray fell like hard rain, and then the Thames spat them out the other side.

Parker looked over the side to see they were six feet above the water, plummeting down toward it.

"Brace." The waterman lifted his oars high but ready, and when they smacked down onto the surface he dipped them in and heaved, propelling the boat forward so the impact did not brake them too much and tip the front into the water.

The relative quiet after the assault under the span gave Parker the sense he had lost his hearing.

"Well, that was a good 'un." The waterman laughed, the sound almost maniacal.

Parker rose a little from his place at the back of the boat, searching for the merchant.

And there he was, urging his waterman toward a small beach on the riverbank.

"There will be no trouble for you," he called out. "I only want some answers."

"I saw your chain of office under your cloak. What do you want? Me in the Tower?" the merchant called back from his boat.

"What have you done, that you should fear the Tower?"

"You were asking after Jens of Antwerp. Do you know what has happened to him? He is dead! And a thousand curses on

him. He has ruined me, brought the life I had here to an end."
His words bounced on the water with an echo.

"What did he want of you?" Parker silently urged his waterman to go faster. They seemed no closer than they had
been, and the merchant was almost to the shore. "I swear in
the King's name, if you answer me truly, I will not stop you
leaving."

The merchant turned in his seat to face Parker. "He
wanted passage on one of my ships. A way to slip out of the
country. But he was not cautious enough. He was followed to
my house, and I was called to answer to the Duke of Norfolk
himself. I am ruined."

"Do you know what trouble Jens was in? Why he needed to
leave so suddenly?"

But the merchant had turned back and was looking at the
shoreline, silent.

Parker followed his line of sight and saw a figure in brown,
hat pulled low, on the high part of the bank. His stomach
dipped, rock-heavy, as he caught sight of the crossbow in the
man's hand.

Someone hailed Parker from the left, and he saw Harry
and Susanna running along the road toward him. Toward the
assassin waiting on the bank.

"Back!" At his shout, the merchant jerked, looking at him
in fear.

But Harry had seen, had grabbed Susanna and was pulling
her toward St. Magnus Church, while the assassin weighed
where to aim his bow. He swung toward her, but there were al-

ready cries and shouts of alarm from the crowds above as they noticed his weapon.

With a final heave, the waterman piloting the merchant's boat scraped the shore, with Parker's boatman just behind them.

"Get below the bank, out of sight." Parker leaped from the boat, diving past the merchant to take the path at a run. But by the time he'd climbed the bank, he could see the Frenchman running toward the crowds of Billingsgate Market, where it would be impossible to catch him.

Harry waved to him from the doorway of St. Magnus. They were safe.

He turned back, walking down to the boats, surprised to see the watermen struggling with the merchant.

He was tired of chasing down leads that ended in nothing, and he strode to where the three men fought and pulled out his knife.

At the sight of it, the merchant stopped his struggles.

"Held on to 'im for ya, sir." The waterman who had piloted his boat gave him a grin, his teeth dark brown stumps in his mouth.

Parker gave a nod of thanks to the watermen and they stepped in front of the boats in case the merchant tried to escape that way.

He hefted his knife and, after a moment, slipped it back up his sleeve. "If you answer me, I will let you take your cart and leave for Dover. If you don't, I will personally deliver you to the Tower myself." He spoke evenly.

The merchant lifted a hand in defeat, then flicked his eyes to the watermen, but they were far enough away to give them a measure of privacy. Even so, the merchant pitched his voice very low.

"I don't know the whole of it. I am glad that I don't. But Jens let one thing slip, and it was then I realized how much trouble he had led me into by his contact." The man shifted his gaze to the bank above, and then dropped his voice even further. "Jens was in London to assess a gem. The Mirror of Naples. I do not know who commissioned him to undertake the task, only that he discovered there was more to the job than merely valuing it and verifying what it was. He would not cooperate with the larger plot, and he and his employer fell out over it. He became a hunted man."

Parker stared at him. "You are sure of this?"

The man nodded.

Parker stepped away, and the merchant cowered back as if expecting him to strike. But Parker was already fumbling for a coin each for the watermen for their help, tossing them through the air to them. He ran back up the narrow path that led to the road, leaving the merchant to his own devices.

Whoever was behind this, if they were trying to steal the Mirror of Naples, then they were surely trying to force the King into war.

# 14

*It is necessary for a prince wishing to hold his own to know how to do wrong, and to make use of it or not according to necessity.*

—*Machiavelli*, The Prince, *chapter 15*

The King was back at Bridewell.

It saved Parker riding out to him, for which he was infinitely grateful.

He kept hold of Susanna as they skirted the chaos of the courtyard, trying to avoid the mud. He shoved a little harder than he usually would against the crush of bodies as he forged a path into the great hall.

A monkey was screeching and chattering, causing cries and yelps as it ran over the heads and shoulders of the servants lifting trunks and chests.

It leaped at Parker, landing on his shoulder and clutching tight to his cloak. Parker could feel it shivering, hopping from side to side with agitation.

Susanna stopped, uncertain, and he grabbed the creature by the scruff of its neck and held it away from her.

"He won't hurt you."

Parker saw Will Somers approaching, stoop-shouldered and gaunt, his face for once free of any mockery.

"Come here, lambkin," Somers said.

Parker held the monkey out and it jumped into Somers's arms and then scuttled to his shoulder, chattering softly in his ear. Somers stroked its golden brown fur with a long, bony finger. "You were frightened by this unholy racket, weren't you, lambkin?"

"Where is the King?" Parker drew Susanna closer as two servants staggered past with a massive chest.

"In his bedchamber, and when he has bathed and changed his clothes, he'll move to the Privy Chamber." Somers bowed to Susanna and then to Parker. "You missed all manner of excitement in the country."

"I have excitement enough of my own. Is the King much harmed?"

Somers shook his head. "He's well enough, thanks to his groom. The lad will be well rewarded for his quick thinking. He jumped down into the mud with His Majesty and pulled him out."

"That must have given you some good material, Fool."

Somers laughed. "I haven't been with the King long enough to make light of his near death." He gave a theatrical wave of his hand. "Although if the King continues so hale, hearty, and energetic, I may yet have the chance."

"I must speak with the King before he moves to the Privy Chamber, so we will take our leave." Parker gave a quick bow, but Somers laid a hand on his arm.

"What trouble have you been stirring up, Parker? The moment the King arrived, Wolsey was in with him, complaining about you."

Parker looked hard at Somers, then at his hand. With exaggerated flourish, Somers lifted it up, extending a finger and giving a little twirl.

"So taciturn. So fierce. I have been here only a month, and already I have learned that you are the one to watch out for. And you are so silent and stealthy, you give me nothing to mock."

Parker still said nothing, and Somers gave a great laugh that rose from his belly. "Ah, how can I deny you? The King has ordered all but his Fool to be banished from his presence while his servants change his clothes, and since you are such a sweet talker, I will get you before him."

"We are much obliged." Susanna curtsied, and Somers looked at her thoughtfully.

Parker drew her even closer. "Lead on, Fool."

———

Henry was being dried. Parker saw his lips drawn into a snarl as he endured the nervous pats of one of his servants of the body, and braced himself for the King's bad mood.

"Your Majesty." Parker bowed.

Henry looked up and some of his irritation faded. "Parker. What news?"

He would have to play this carefully. "There is something afoot, I fear."

Henry lost his scowl completely and rubbed his hands together. "Ah. Tell me. I am in dire need of distraction from my troubles."

"This may add to them." Parker kept his eyes on the King's face.

Henry laughed, a bitter, hard sound. "They are so heavy now, I don't expect a little extra weight will make much difference." He stepped into fresh body linen and gave Parker a nod to continue.

"I think we should have this discussion alone, Your Majesty." Parker knew Norfolk's habit of insinuating spies into the King's service, and Wolsey was known for doing the same. None of the listening ears in this room could be trusted.

"Out then, all of you."

Parker held out a robe for the King to put on while the room emptied.

Henry shrugged into it and sat beside the fire, and for the first time, Parker thought the weight of rule rested heavily on his shoulders.

"Are you truly well from the fall?"

"Aye. In body, I am fine. It is the squabbling over who will succeed me if I should die that makes me sick of spirit."

"What will you do?" There were only a few options open to the King, and none of them would make everyone happy.

"I think to make Fitzroy a Knight of the Garter. Elevate him, prepare him. He has not the legitimacy of Mary, but he is a boy. The nobles will not take well to a woman on the throne."

"It is a problem." Parker eased into a chair beside the King.

Henry snorted. "My one child is a girl, the other is a bastard. Katherine will not bear me another." He stared into the fire. "I can hear the howls of the dogs closing in on me." Then he roused himself. "What is this secret news?"

"I have stumbled upon a plot. I am not sure of it, but it may be the French are trying to steal the Mirror of Naples. Either as a ransom payment to the Emperor for the return of the French king, or to restore France's pride."

Henry stared at him, openmouthed. "They would steal the Mirror of Naples? From me?"

Parker turned his gaze to the fire. "Some may say they were simply stealing it back."

Henry let out a laugh. "Some may. They may even be right, but they'd better not say it in my hearing." He tapped a fist on his thigh. "If they succeed, we would look foolish. Even with their king captured, they would have bested us."

"Aye." Parker rose up. "With your permission I would see the jewel, see where it is kept and what can be done to safeguard it."

"Speak to Wyatt. He's the Master of the King's Jewels." Henry rose as well. "What alerted you to this, Parker?"

"An assassin, Your Majesty."

"An assassin?" Henry's eyes widened.

"A man who has killed one of the most important witnesses to the plot and has dogged my heels, trying to silence the others."

"A marksman?"

"The best I have ever encountered." Parker went to the door.

Henry watched him from the fire, and there was a new awareness in his eyes. This was no longer a distraction from his succession troubles. "Watch your back, then."

"I intend to."

# 15

*A wise prince should establish himself on that which is in his own control and not in that of others.*

—Machiavelli, The Prince, *chapter 17*

Susanna flexed her fingers and rued her lack of charcoal and paper.

Somers and his monkey were watching her, looming over her seat in the passageway outside the King's chambers, and she wondered what he would say if she asked to draw him. His cheekbones were as prominent as the haunches of a starving cow, and he had the tall, stooped appearance of Death itself.

Parker had been unwilling to leave her, but even he conceded the King was not likely to welcome a woman into his bedchamber while he was dressing.

"I will let no harm befall her," Somers had offered before Parker could even make the request, and he'd given a sharp nod and gone through the doors, as if not to waste a minute.

"What delights have you been up to today, my lady?"

Susanna laughed. "The delights of watching some boating on the Thames."

"Ah, there is a story there, I can tell." Somers rubbed his hands together, but Susanna shook her head.

"Not one that can be repeated."

Somers turned his mouth and eyes down at the corners as if to cry. "It is a good thing most courtiers are not so mean with the details, my lady. I would have nothing to occupy me."

Susanna smiled. "I'm sure you have enough, without ours."

"I get by." Somers spoke deadpan, and Susanna smiled again.

She was sure he did more than get by in the viper pit that was the court. She had never met him before today, but now she understood how he'd become the King's favorite so quickly. He seemed to take excitement with him—the promise of laughter clung to him as tightly as his monkey on his shoulder. Something Henry would find infinitely appealing.

"Ho, Somers." A man walked toward them, his eyes bright and intelligent. And curious.

She saw him look at her sidelong, as if he were embarrassed to acknowledge her directly.

She had no such qualms herself. He was magnificent; handsome enough to make girls swoon. His hair curled over his shoulders in a fair wave, and she didn't doubt he had but to crook a finger to have a lady on each arm.

Somers clicked his tongue like an admonishing mother. "Do you have no courtly manners, Wyatt? I'm sure I've seen you bow prettily to the ladies a time or two. Why do you not do so to the beauty beside me?"

Wyatt blushed, and Susanna liked him immediately.

"I beg your pardon, madame, I thought . . ." His words trailed off and his blush seemed to deepen.

"He thought you were perhaps waiting for an audience with our half-clothed Majesty, eh?" Somers rolled his eyes and Susanna blushed herself.

This was not the first time she had been mistaken for one of the King's mistresses. Most of the Queen's ladies in waiting had taken her for such only a month ago. Even the King's current mistress had taken her for a rival.

Somers took pity on them. "My lady, this mannerless cur is the poet and layabout Thomas Wyatt. Wyatt, I present the King's painter, Mistress Horenbout. My lady is Parker's betrothed."

Wyatt bowed very low. "Forgive me, my lady. I have been away from court for a time, and though I had heard the King had a beautiful and talented painter, and that Parker had swooped like the hawk he is and snatched her for himself, I have not had the pleasure of seeing you before."

Somers rolled his eyes again and Susanna dipped her head in acknowledgment.

"I heard you were away, trying to make a certain lady of the court happier about her banishment to the country." Somers's voice was sly, yet light and teasing at the same time. It was difficult to dislike him.

Wyatt looked at him with annoyance. "You have the ears

of an elephant, Fool. Where do you come by your information?"

"Oh, there is plenty of talk, especially since Lady Anne almost got Percy to break his betrothal in order to marry her."

"Anne Boleyn is no schemer." Wyatt seemed outraged at the suggestion. "She was in love with Percy. She's fuming that Wolsey had her sent away from court for following her heart."

Susanna stiffened at the mention of the name Boleyn, and she caught Somers watching her with a knowing expression.

"Mistress Horenbout does not like the Boleyn family. Am I right?"

In this one thing, when it came to the Boleyns, Susanna was not prepared to play the courtly game of courtesy and denial. "I do not. As you must know why, I'm sure you don't blame me."

"What wrong has Anne done to you?" Wyatt gaped at her, aghast.

"None. It is her brother I do not like."

Wyatt frowned. "What has George done—"

He cut off suddenly at the look on her face, and flushed.

"I know he is sometimes less . . . genteel than he should be when it comes to women."

"He sees"—Somers lifted an open palm level with his eyes—"and he takes." He threw his hand forward, closing it into a fist.

"He will not attempt to take my betrothed again." Parker was suddenly beside them. "Unless he wishes to die by my hand."

"Or mine." Susanna spoke quietly, but all three men heard her. Somers looked interested; Wyatt's eyes widened in shock.

"Wyatt, you have saved me some time. Come with me." Although Parker spoke to Wyatt, he looked only at her. He put out a hand to her and Susanna took it, heart thundering, as he pulled her to her feet. He had a way of looking at her, intense and exciting, that could make the rest of the room fade to nothing.

"I'm afraid I need to speak with the King, Parker, about a matter—"

"The King is taking no audience now, Wyatt. And his orders are that your father assist me." There was not the smallest bend in Parker's tone, and Wyatt took a step back.

"Aye? Then of course I am your man."

"Good. Let us discuss our business elsewhere."

Somers's gaze darted between them with growing delight. "Now what could this be?"

Parker looked at him steadily, and the Fool rose to his feet and laughed. "I'm leaving, Parker; I'm leaving." He minced away, his monkey's tail swishing irritably from his shoulder, and just before he turned down the passageway, he gave a little wave.

"What is afoot?" Wyatt cocked his head.

"I need to see one of the King's jewels."

Wyatt moved uncomfortably. "To have it reset?"

Parker shook his head. "To make sure it's still there."

# 16

The Mirror of Naples was gone.

Wyatt stared down at the empty cask in the jewel house at Westminster, his face ashen. "Perhaps my father is having it cleaned, or has put it elsewhere."

Parker reached out a hand and fingered the untampered lock. "You are the Clerk of the King's Jewels; your father is the Master. You would know if a jewel of this importance was out of its cask for any reason, as part of your duties."

Wyatt hesitated a moment. "My father and I are not always in the best of humors with each other. He thinks I should try harder with my marriage, that I should behave more chastely with other women because of my marriage vows." Wyatt fiddled with the sleeves of his doublet. "He was furious with me for leaving London two weeks ago to return to our country estate. It is possible he made arrangements for the jewel without out my knowledge."

Wyatt was lying. The tremble of his hands, the fine line of perspiration on his lip, gave him away.

Parker tapped his lips. "Why did you leave London two weeks ago?"

Wyatt started. "Anne Boleyn, whose family estate neighbors my own family holdings, was sent home by Wolsey some weeks ago. I went to keep company with her, cheer her up."

"Why did Wolsey have her sent away?" Perhaps he should try harder to listen to court gossip, but he never had the patience for it.

Wyatt clenched a fist and turned away. "She formed an attachment to a young courtier, Percy, but he was already betrothed. When he asked his father to break the betrothal to marry Anne, Wolsey had Anne sent home, and his father married him to his betrothed before the week was out." His voice was bitter as chicory, and Parker thought Wyatt a man who was made for ripe peaches.

"You are fond of Mistress Boleyn." Susanna spoke as if stating a fact. She held a piece of parchment, the inventory, if Parker was any judge, and had rolled it open.

Wyatt nodded. "If I could have chosen whom to wed . . ." He looked out the window.

"What does the jewel look like?" Susanna ran a finger down the list in her hand.

"It is a diamond as long as a man's middle finger, with a massive pearl dangling from it." Wyatt spoke tonelessly.

"And His Majesty somehow took it from the King of France?" Susanna frowned. "How could that be?"

Parker exchanged a look with Wyatt. "His sister, Mary, received it as part of her bridal gifts when she became Queen of France. When she was widowed, she took it, although it was part of the French crown jewels and not hers to take. She gave it to Henry as a way to make things right with him."

"Make things right? What did she do?"

There was a moment of silence. This was not a story told in public. It could land the teller in trouble. Parker leaned back against the wall, and when he spoke, his voice was low. "The King sent his best friend, Charles Brandon, to fetch Mary back to England when Louis died. Mary had long been in love with Brandon, and she insisted that they marry in France without her brother's permission, before Henry could use her in another diplomatic marriage. To avoid Henry's fury at their outrageous behavior, she presented him with the Mirror of Naples. The nobles were calling for Brandon's head on the block, but Henry was mollified enough by the payment of a hefty fine, and the diamond, to forgive them."

"They say it is better to ask forgiveness than to ask permission and be denied." Wyatt's voice was as soft as Parker's had been. "Percy has learned that the hard way. If he'd had the courage, he could have married Anne and there would have been nothing his father or Wolsey could have done."

"But then Anne would not be free." Susanna spoke just as softly.

"I cannot have her anyway. She is determined to marry well, not become some married man's mistress."

And Wyatt had had his share of mistresses.

Parker liked him, had felt faintly sorry for him. His wife was habitually unfaithful, matching him conquest for conquest, and Parker always thought Wyatt rather tragic. More handsome than any man had a right to be, yet trapped with a woman not of his choosing who reacted to his lack of love by cuckolding him at every opportunity. They had but one child together, a very young boy.

Something rose out of his memory. "How is your son?"

Wyatt blinked. "He is well, last I saw him, which was two weeks ago, before I left London."

"Norfolk is the boy's godfather, is he not?"

Wyatt went still. "Aye. A very generous godfather."

"And he is your patron, too, I recall."

Wyatt swallowed. "What has this to do with the missing jewel?"

"The Mirror of Naples isn't just a jewel." Parker kept his eyes on Wyatt's face. "To the King, it is a badge of honor. He wears it, and everyone remembers that it should be with the crown jewels of France. Yet there it sits, on his robes. And it reminds all who see it that Henry calls himself King of France, as well as England. That he considers it his by right."

Wyatt was silent.

"So when did you discover the Mirror of Naples was missing, Wyatt?" Parker slammed the cask lid down with a crack, and Wyatt jumped. "And when did you go running to Norfolk about it, instead of telling the King?"

---

Wyatt sat slumped on a cask, his head in his hands, and Susanna wished she could paint him just so. He was the perfect model for a tragic hero.

She realized her thoughts were coldhearted, but his friendship with the Boleyns had cooled her liking for him, although she knew friendships formed in youth were very forgiving, almost blind, as one grew older.

He would see George as he was in his childhood, not what he'd become.

If her thoughts were coldhearted, the way Parker was looking at Wyatt was positively icy. Wyatt caught his gaze and flinched away.

"This is a mess." Wyatt spoke as if from the bottom of a pit. "When I found the Mirror was missing, I told Norfolk because I wanted revenge on Wolsey. I never thought it would drag on this long. I never counted on someone discovering the jewel was missing before Norfolk had gathered his evidence against Wolsey."

"You suspect Wolsey of taking the jewel?" Parker crouched down in front of Wyatt and Susanna thought he was going to take him by the shoulders and shake the answers out of him.

"Aye. He is responsible, I am sure of it. But there is no direct path back to him." Wyatt closed his eyes in misery.

"And the indirect path?" Susanna sat on a cask herself.

"He claimed to be updating the inventory." Wyatt flicked his head in the direction of the scroll Susanna held in her hands. "Which was my father's and my responsibility. It was a slight to my father and he was outraged. Wolsey said it was to readjust the values recorded. He brought in a diamond cutter from Antwerp to make the assessments. To evaluate the clarity and the number of carats of each piece."

"Jens of Antwerp?" Parker looked across to Susanna.

"No." Wyatt looked up at last, surprised. "He gave us the name of Pieter Diamantaire. He spent every day for two weeks here. This was three weeks ago. I didn't trust anyone sent by Wolsey and kept coming in to watch him work. My father did the same. But he appeared to know his business."

"Did he have a blue cloak?" Susanna nervously turned the inventory in her hands, and then made her fingers still. The worst had already happened.

"Aye. A fine blue cloak. I complimented him upon it."

"And when did you notice the Mirror was gone?" Parker's voice was cool as the air blowing in at the windows.

"The day he left. I checked the boxes as soon as he was gone. I could have started anywhere, but the Mirror was the first box I opened." He patted his heart, remembering. "For one terrible moment, I thought perhaps every box would be empty. But it was the only one."

"And you ran to Norfolk." The chill again. "And then ran and hid in the country."

"I *knew* Wolsey was behind it. I *knew* it. And I wanted the bastard to pay. I was in more of a temper with him than usual because of sending Anne away, and Norfolk, it seems, is in more of a temper with him than usual because of some grant he's issued. He bypassed Parliament and simply sent it out, as if there is no law in England but his own."

"And then there is the fact the King's most prized jewel went missing under your nose." Susanna didn't know why she threw that barb, but the Boleyns and Norfolk had that effect on her. Even though she had no love for Wolsey, they had done her more wrong than he.

Wyatt raised his head, and there was surprise and hurt in his eyes. "Aye. It went missing under my nose. But Wolsey was responsible. I was not careless. I know that will not save me with the King, but I was not negligent. Wolsey will make sure I look so when he speaks to the King against me. I went to Norfolk, trusted him, and he has delayed it too long. He has not found the Mirror and he has found no evidence against Wolsey. So I cannot go to the King now without looking guilty. Without perhaps being considered a traitor to the Crown."

Susanna studied the inventory again, a little shamed. She traced a note, written in French next to one of the pieces listed, with the tip of her finger. Jens had written this, nervous in his subterfuge, going by a false name. He must have truly thought no one he knew would see him, recognize him. He could return to Antwerp and none would even know where he'd been.

She saw that he had marked figures, prices, weights, and clarity next to a large number of the items on the list. He had written a note only next to the one, though.

Had he truly done the job Wolsey claimed he'd been brought here to do? If she knew Jens, even if it were a pretense, he would not have lied in the inventory. The carats and values he'd written would be correct.

But this had all been three weeks ago. Why had he stayed in London?

Perhaps Jens had decided to come clean and tell the truth, had threatened to expose the Cardinal?

Susanna dismissed the idea. The Mirror had already been taken. Jens had only to get on a boat to the Netherlands and be free.

Even with his clumsy attempt to kill her, he could have gotten away with it. She lived in London now. He would be able to avoid her for the rest of his life, and probably still keep the friendship of her father if he swore it hadn't been him, that she had confused him with someone else.

"Whatever you have done, nothing can change it." Parker's tone to Wyatt was softer than it had been. "But from now on, if you hear anything, notice anything, you come to me. Not Norfolk. If I hear of you approaching him, I'll throw you to the King and watch him tear you up."

Wyatt dragged fine, long-fingered hands through his beautiful hair. "You always were a bastard, Parker." He stood.

"I wouldn't forget that, if I were you." Parker stood beside him, a dark angel to Wyatt's light.

Although there was a place inside Parker as dark as his outer shell, there was also a purity to him, an ability to be happy, that Susanna thought Wyatt might lack.

Again, she wished for her paints. She could see it in her mind's eye: the dark as steady, a sure, solid color. The light as flickering, wavering, inconsistent.

Wyatt held out his hand for the inventory.

"As I am here, I will see to some duties that have been neglected these last two weeks."

Parker gave a shallow bow. "You know where to find me, if you have anything to say."

Wyatt nodded and Parker held out his arm for Susanna to take.

The door closed behind them as if Wyatt had kicked it shut, and she smiled at Parker. "You always make so many friends."

He smiled back, lifted her hand, and kissed it. "A man can never have too many."

"What do you think Wolsey is up to?"

"I think he knew what we scrambled to uncover a month ago, all along. He knew about de la Pole's army planning its invasion of England, and about the secret alliance France signed with the current pope, giving the King of France more influence in Rome.

So I believe Cardinal Wolsey's plan was to exchange the Mirror of Naples for the French king's promise of the highest seat in the Church. He would become pope."

# 17

*Those who solely by good fortune become princes from
being private citizens have little trouble in rising, but
much in keeping atop; they have not any difficulties on
the way up, because they fly, but they have many when
they reach the summit.*

—Machiavelli, The Prince, *chapter 7*

Parker wanted to find some deep, dark cave to hide Susanna.

The house would have to do.

He polished the crossbow set between his knees, rubbing
oil into the fine-grained wood. He couldn't protect her until
he'd killed the assassin. And he didn't even know to whom
the man answered.

Not Norfolk, unless the Duke was playing an even more
twisted game than usual. It might be Wolsey—but the way
he'd come undone at the mention of the Frenchman, Parker
thought not.

The emissaries of the French court were a possibility. If this
was an official bargain between Wolsey and King Francis, then

the assassin might have been sent by the French to make sure no word of the plan got out.

Nothing would bring Henry to war faster than knowledge of a plot to steal the Mirror of Naples. No matter what reason Henry gave officially, it would be a matter of pride with him.

There was a sound at the door and Susanna stepped into the room, her hair unbound and spilling over her shoulders, her eyes shadowed.

"You are going out?" She looked at the crossbow, and he could see the weight on her shoulders increase.

"Not until much later."

She frowned. "It is already late."

"Aye, but I wish to wake men up, not visit them while they are feasting and making merry."

He set aside the crossbow and held out a hand to her.

She came to him as she always did, without hesitation.

"I worry about you." She slid onto his lap and whispered the words into his ear as he pulled her close.

He brushed a hand through her hair, smoothing it back and then tangling his fingers deep in it, relishing the fragrance of rosemary that rose up. "It isn't safe for you to go outside until I've killed him."

Susanna shook her head. "He knows we won't keep whatever Jens or the merchant said to ourselves. If he has spies, or if he followed us, he'll know we've been to the King. He won't waste his time on us now."

"Perhaps. But I will not risk you on that gamble." And if Susanna was right, if he thought the King had enough information to move on him, the assassin might be about to flee the country.

Parker didn't want to give him a chance to run.

"I've been thinking—" Susanna shifted in his arms, laid her head against his shoulder. "Why was the assassin on the banks of the Thames this afternoon looking to kill either me or the merchant, if the Mirror has already been stolen?"

Parker began to stroke her neck. "Because until someone raises the alarm, it is merely not where it should be. Jens was only killed two days ago. Wolsey must have kept Jens in London to be able to produce him should any finger be pointed back to himself, yet surely Jens would only agree to that if the jewel could be to hand at a moment's notice. He would face execution if the jewel was gone and he was the only suspect."

"You think the gem has been hidden, awaiting arrangements?" She leaned back into his hand and he increased the pressure of his fingers, felt the stiffness in her shoulders loosen a little.

"Wolsey would not risk stealing from his only protector without an ironclad guarantee from the French."

"But something happened," Susanna said.

"Yes, something happened. It must have taken Wolsey months to arrange for Jens to come to London, for everything to fall into place. And then, the King of France was captured. The alliance with the Pope abandoned."

"Perhaps he went ahead with it anyway? Still hoping?"

"It's possible he couldn't abandon it. It was the path to

his life's ambition." Parker played with the ties at Susanna's neck.

"And the French, knowing the jewel is ready for them, are pushing for it." She made a humming noise in the back of her throat. It rubbed against his skin like velvet. "They have spent so long arranging for its return, they can't leave the prize when it's so close."

"And Jens would not divulge where he had hidden the Mirror to the assassin. He may not have known where it was." Parker undid a tie.

"And Wolsey?" She glanced at him as he slid his fingers inside her dress.

"They are intimidating him. Perhaps threatening to blackmail him." Parker thought of what Gittens had told him. "I'm sure he's receiving visits from the assassin himself. They are squeezing him, pounding him down, to get the Mirror back." His voice trailed away as the softness of her skin distracted him.

She brought her lips to his, a whisper away. "I thought you were going out."

"I will." He slid his hand deeper inside her gown. "Later."

# 18

*Therefore it is unnecessary for a prince to have all the good qualities I have enumerated, but it is very necessary to appear to have them.*

—Machiavelli, The Prince, *chapter 18*

The nobleman who conducted business on behalf of the French king lived well, Parker observed, as he stood outside the count's massive stone house.

Like a flickering candle stub, a party fought for life in the large dining room, its window too high off the ground for Parker to look through without the aid of a crate or step. He could hear a few shouts of laughter, followed by long silences, and guessed the guests who remained were holding on to the bitter end at this late hour.

A stablehand brought two bays from the back, their shoes clicking on the gray stone path, and Parker edged deeper into shadows. Perhaps the last of them were leaving, if they'd called for their horses.

The stablehand shivered in the cold, and the horses blew and fidgeted, annoyed with being taken from a warm stable. The boy whispered to them, rubbing their necks and calming them.

Parker wondered if the last guests had passed out, to keep their horses waiting. He lost patience and stepped to the front door. It swung open with a creak and the stable boy's head jerked up.

Parker gave him a salute before he slipped inside.

The hall was dark and just outside the dining room, an exhausted servant tried to lift a guest up from a pool of vomit. Through the half-open door, voices were raised in heated conversation.

Parker watched the servant lift the man's head, then drop it back in the puddle of sick. He seemed unaware of Parker, his eyes deeply shadowed. He turned and shuffled down the passage, small and stooped.

The smell in the hallway was choking, and Parker stepped over the prone man, angled through the door, and entered the room beyond.

Two men turned in his direction. Another guest lay sprawled across the long table, his cheek nestled in a dish.

"Which of you owns the horses outside?" Parker saw their eyes widen at the question. It was not what they were expecting.

One of the men standing moved slightly, as if in confirmation.

"They are taking a chill." Parker pointed in the direction

of the courtyard. "I wouldn't want to keep such fine horses waiting; it isn't good for them."

The man held a hand over one eye, as if to see Parker better, then sidled toward the door, muttering under his breath as he weaved his way out.

Parker turned to the one who was left. "Are you the Comte, or is he?" Parker pointed to the man passed out on the table.

"*C'est moi.*" The man pulled himself up, then staggered to the side. "I am he."

"You have someone working for you. A man who favors a crossbow."

The Comte put out a hand and grasped the back of a chair, his knuckles white with effort. "*Non.*"

"Yes. In the last three days he has killed a man, and tried to kill a few more. My betrothed is on his list."

The Comte shook his head, the movement making him dizzy enough to need a second hand on the chair to steady himself. His lips worked as if he were trying to find the words to deny it, but he said nothing.

"I would have a word with your man. Immediately."

The Comte shook his head again, winced, and began to edge away.

Parker moved, adder-quick. He still had the feel of Susanna on his skin, the deep green scent of rosemary, the smooth curves of her body. He would not have her threatened another moment.

In two steps he had the Comte lying across the table, his head resting on the lip of a plate of roast pheasant.

"Where is he?"

"He is dangerous, monsieur. You do not want to find this man."

"You are wrong. I want to find him very badly."

The Comte looked up with flat eyes. "I cannot tell you. I know him. He will kill you, then he will kill me. And if by some miracle you manage to kill him first, then my king will kill me when I return."

"I will make this easy for you." Parker lifted his knife and placed it just below the Comte's right eye, so he could see it if he looked down.

"You will not get the Mirror back. You do not wish for a war with England while your king is a prisoner of the Emperor. But you will get one if you continue this madness."

"You can arrange a war all on your own, can you?" The Comte's mouth turned in a sneer, and his gaze was no longer on the blade against his cheek but on Parker's face.

"Aye. I can do just that." Parker spoke with quiet conviction. "It will not be difficult to convince my king to do that which he is already considering."

The Comte looked away, down the table to where the last guest lay snoring into a dish of pastries.

"Perhaps the clever thing would be to make sure you don't get the chance?" The Comte turned back, his eyes blazing with triumph.

The smug look of victory was a mistake.

As Parker heard the crack of glass smashing, he lifted his arm and threw his knife at the guest who had risen, cake mashed into his cheek, a jagged wine bottle drawn back to throw.

He dived left, too late, and the thud of the jagged bottle into his flesh was the only sound he could hear. White-hot pain seared down his arm, and then the shouts of the Comte pierced the thrumming of blood in his ears. A man screamed in agony, and something dropped to the floor with a clatter.

His knife?

Parker gritted his teeth and snaked under the table to retrieve it, sliding in blood.

It was not all his.

He rose cautiously, gripping the table. The assassin stood at an open window, panting, his face white against the night sky. He pressed a hand to his upper shoulder, blood staining his fingers, and Parker looked down and saw the bottle still buried high on his own right shoulder.

He pulled it out by the neck, refusing to make a sound, then lifted his gaze to the window again, knife ready. But the assassin was gone.

Parker looked after him, swaying. Then he blinked to clear his vision and turned to the door.

"Where are you going?" The Comte was still crouched by the table, his words a whisper.

Parker glanced at him. "Perhaps to start a war."

He threw the bottle, dripping with his blood, at the Comte's feet.

He looked like a Viking from the old sagas. Wild-eyed, blood stiff in his hair, caking his clothes.

A dark stain sat high on his shoulder.

He held his knife in one hand, as if he'd carried it across London, expecting immediate attack.

Susanna had run into the hallway when she heard him on the front steps, and she stumbled to a stop, staring, as he closed the door behind him.

He watched her, waiting to see what she would do. A spray of blood, fine as the pattern on a butterfly's wing, decorated the ridge of his cheek.

She felt a cry well up within her chest and she fought it, fought the way it wanted to twist her face, her mouth, and fill her eyes with tears.

She went to him, gentle, careful, and he bent his face to hers. She kissed his lips lightly. She was too afraid to put her arms around him.

"Can you walk to the study?"

He nodded and she expected him to use her shoulder to lean on, but he walked under his own power, then sank down beside the fire.

"I will get Peter Jack to call Maggie."

He started to protest, but she ignored him and walked out of the room to the kitchen.

Peter Jack was already yawning and stumbling out of his room, roused by the sound of voices at the door.

"Fetch Maggie."

He froze mid-stretch and his gaze went to the passageway. "Bad?"

"Bad enough." Susanna went straight to the hearth and took a jug to scoop up some hot water from the pot in the embers.

Peter Jack had his boots on and his cloak about him by the time she had stoked the fire.

"Bolt wound?" he asked.

She shook her head, viciously stamping down the wail inside her, pressing her lips together and gulping as it tried to claw its way up.

"Broken bottle."

The door slammed behind Peter Jack as he ran out, and she took a deep breath, trying to still her hands as she fumbled through a drawer for some clean cloths.

Then she picked up the jug of water and walked carefully out of the room, watching to make sure she did not spill.

There would be no more spilling tonight. No water, no tears.

No blood.

# 19

*Every one sees what you appear to be, few really know what you are, and those few dare not oppose themselves to the opinion of the many, who have the majesty of the state to defend them; and in the actions of all men, and especially of princes, which it is not prudent to challenge, one judges by the result.*

—Machiavelli, The Prince, *chapter 25*

It was like old days, Parker thought. He would get into trouble, and Maggie would patch him up.

She glared at him now, stirring something with a little pestle. "I thought this kind of thing was over, when you became a fine gentleman for the King."

Parker looked down at his shirt lying on the floor, cut to ribbons, and at the deep cuts in his shoulder. "The King's business is not all courtly dances and days at the joust."

Maggie snorted. Her tiny sylph of an assistant stepped forward with a jug of water, and Maggie held the mortar out for her to pour in a splash.

"Will it heal well?" Susanna sounded as though she were fighting something when she spoke. Every word was measured.

"Aye." Maggie looked disgusted, as if she'd hoped it were otherwise. "Nothing important was damaged, and he can feel down his arm to his fingertips, so he should make a full recovery if he keeps it clean." She lifted up some of the mixture in the mortar with a spoon and dropped a little onto Parker's shoulder.

It was hot and it stung, and Parker swallowed a curse.

"Keep putting this on every few hours," Maggie told Susanna. She packed her things in quick, deft movements. "I get far too much business from this house." She sniffed, and slung her bag over her shoulder. "Lock him up if you have to." Then, with her assistant in tow, she sailed from the room.

Parker closed his eyes, riding out the sting of the herb paste on his wound. He heard Maggie go through the kitchen and have a word with Mistress Greene, who'd woken when Peter Jack had returned with the healer. The house was a blaze of light, and it was not yet matins. The bells of St. Michael's would not ring for a few more hours.

The room was silent. The small sounds Susanna made as she gathered the jug of water and cloths she'd used to mop the blood from his shoulder had ceased, and he opened his eyes.

She stood in the middle of the room, her hands full, tears streaming down her cheeks.

He felt his heart rip.

"My love." He pushed out of his chair, forgetting his shoulder and staggering under the sudden stab of pain.

Susanna dropped the jug with a clatter, pressing her hands to her mouth as if to still the trembling of her lips.

"I am safe and well." He slid his arms around her, wincing as the movement caused ripples of pain up his neck and down his arm.

She said nothing, shaking in the circle of his arms without making a sound. His left hand stroked her back, and at last she breathed in deeply and lifted her head.

"This cannot go on. It needs to end." She spoke in a whisper.

"I drew blood from him tonight. He will not easily lift a crossbow for a few days. It will give us some time."

She sighed and rested her head against his left shoulder. "What is Norfolk's role in this, do you think?"

Parker let the feel of her, the heat and flexible strength, seep into his tired body. "When Wyatt went to him about the Mirror, it was surely the best day of Norfolk's life. If he could expose Wolsey to the King, catch him out with the Mirror of Naples . . ." Parker thought of the humiliation, the absolute disgrace that would come down on Wolsey. "It would be the triumph of Norfolk's life at court."

"Norfolk must have had Jens followed, and through that, found the cloth merchant Jens had asked to provide passage out of England." Susanna eased away and led him like a child back to his chair.

"Aye." Parker sank down gratefully. "Jens was either charged by Wolsey to be the courier of the Mirror to France, and was arranging passage with the merchant, or he had some other plan afoot. Perhaps he had even decided to flee without Wolsey's knowledge."

Susanna rubbed her temples. "And Norfolk was either paying or blackmailing the merchant to give him information. To betray Jens."

"To catch Wolsey." Parker closed his eyes. "Norfolk would not care who he ruined if it meant having Wolsey thrown from court. Or better yet, beheaded."

"So what happens now?" Susanna knelt beside him and took his hand in hers.

"The French don't have the Mirror. The Comte would have left with it already if they did. So either Wolsey has it, or he knows where it is. I'll have to talk with him again."

"What happens if he won't tell you?" She traced the back of his hand with her fingertips.

Parker opened his eyes. "He will."

---

Wolsey's red cardinal's hat stood high and proud on his head. When it had been sent from Rome more than ten years earlier, Parker had heard it was received at Dover like royalty and accompanied to London in the same way. There had been a procession through the streets with it.

Now it dipped and swayed as Wolsey stood at the altar in the chapel at Blackfriars. If rumor was right, the Queen had insisted on this ceremony to thank God for sparing the King's life after his fall into the ditch.

Her motives were no doubt sincere, but Parker knew the King did not want any reminders to the nobility that he could have died without a legitimate male heir. The only way to mitigate the damage was to keep it private and quiet. So though the Queen had wanted it held at St. Paul's or Westminster, the King had persuaded her he would prefer a more personal, heartfelt ceremony among friends.

Parker and Susanna's invitation now gave Parker access to Wolsey, if he could get the Cardinal alone.

Quiet ceremony or no, Wolsey had made use of the occasion to wear his red robes, to remind those present that he was the highest-ranking official of Rome in England.

*And you want to be higher.* Parker watched Wolsey perform the rituals and wondered if he would ever attain his ambition. He was one of the King's new men; like Parker himself, raised up from obscurity because of his ambition, intelligence, and hard work. They could have been natural allies, but Wolsey's ego would suffer no rival. Parker had learned long ago that every honor that went to someone else, Wolsey considered stolen from him. He would have it all, even control of the Christian realm itself.

Wolsey came to the end of his liturgy, and the congregation rose.

The King and Queen led the procession out of the chapel, and as he followed, Parker saw tables had been laid in the gallery that connected Bridewell to Blackfriars over the Fleet River. Dishes of small tarts and pies, confectionery and fruit, gleamed in the mid-morning light.

Parker winced as he was jostled in the crowd leaving the chapel and Susanna's hand tightened on his arm. "Is your wound troubling you?"

He dipped his head, keeping his voice for her ear alone. "I would rather no one know of it. Say nothing."

He stumbled as a hand landed heavily on his shoulder, right over his injury.

For a moment he thought he would faint. He saw Susanna's eyes widen and she stepped close into him, her arms going about him as if in embrace. Holding him up.

"I am not sure how things are done in foreign courts, but in England, we behave with decorum in the King's company." The speaker was Thomas Boleyn. Even with spots dancing before his eyes, Parker felt Susanna stiffen against him. As the sharp pain ebbed, he stepped back a little from her. Her nostrils were flared in challenge.

"Is that so?" She could have breathed icy patterns on the gallery's fine glass windows, so cold was her voice. "I am from the court of Margaret of Austria, my lord, and you can draw what conclusions you will from that."

It was Boleyn's turn to stiffen. His face grew flushed, the color rising up from his neck and staining his cheeks red.

Susanna could have let it go there, but she was too furious. Perhaps because it had been Boleyn's hand on Parker that had caused him pain, as well as Boleyn's son who had twice tried to rape her. She drew herself up. "Both your daughter and your son were at court with me there, of course, although your son was sent away for unbecoming behavior, and your daughter—"

"Parker." Boleyn's voice cut Susanna off with the finality of a headman's ax. "I would have an urgent word." He gave a shallow bow in Susanna's direction, devoid of any emotion. "Excuse us, madame."

Parker bowed deeply to her and raised her hand to his lips. Her expression showed clearly what she thought of Boleyn. His mouth twitched as he straightened to join Boleyn to the side of the gathering.

They found a spot a little away from the others, next to a window where the river below them masked their voices.

"What is it?"

Boleyn stepped in close. "There is a rumor you can bring down Wolsey."

Parker stared at him, his mind working. Boleyn was no close friend of Norfolk's. How had he caught wind of this?

Then he remembered where Wyatt had run after he'd found the Mirror was missing: to Anne Boleyn.

# 20

*To appear merciful, faithful, humane, religious, upright, and to be so, but with a mind so framed that should you require not to be so, you may be able and know how to change to the opposite.*

—Machiavelli, The Prince, *chapter 18*

Whatever Boleyn was saying to Parker, Parker did not look happy to hear it. Susanna watched the two men in the alcove, their heads together.

"My lady. I have not seen you these many weeks."

Susanna turned and came face-to-face with Elizabeth Carew. She curtsied, and as she sank down, she wondered if the beauty was still the King's current mistress.

"I have been able to do the King's work mostly in my own rooms, not in the palace." She rose up and found herself again captivated by the woman. "I would like to paint you, my lady, when you have time to sit for me."

The request had sprung from her unbidden, and from the way Elizabeth Carew's mouth fell open, it was the last thing she expected to hear.

"Paint me?"

"Aye." There was no sense going back now. "The scene I have in mind is a stream, deep in a forest, with you rising from the waters."

Elizabeth seemed more startled still. "Not a portrait, then?"

Susanna shook her head.

"I . . . don't know. I will speak with my husband about it."

"That would be most kind."

Elizabeth shifted uncomfortably. "I had hoped . . . that is, I came to ask if you might draw me as you drew Lady Browne in the Queen's chambers last month. I would send the picture to my mother." She clasped her hands in front of her, and Susanna realized Elizabeth had not expected a friendly welcome.

She recalled the way Elizabeth Carew had first treated her, when she'd thought Susanna was the King's new mistress, come to replace her. And felt sorry for her.

"I would be happy to make such a drawing."

"My thanks. Perhaps we can arrange for it next week?" There was a strain to Elizabeth, a brittleness about her that made Susanna think of a fine piece of porcelain. She would shatter if she so much as stumbled.

This court seemed to grab hold of beauties and suck the life from them until their bones lay too close to the surface.

"I am sorry I do not have my charcoals and parchment with me right now." Sunlight streamed into the gallery; it was a good place to draw.

The crowds parted a little, and she saw that Wolsey stood

at the King's shoulder. Henry must have seen him there, but ignored him as he spoke with the Queen and some of her ladies.

Despite the King's clear message, Wolsey remained where he was, swaying from side to side. Susanna thought the movement unconscious. Wolsey was beside himself with agitation or nerves.

"That man." Elizabeth's eyes flared at the sight of the Cardinal. "He tries to oust my brother and husband from the King's circle at every opportunity. He wants only his own men around the King."

Susanna watched Henry clap Elizabeth's brother, Francis Bryan, warmly on the shoulder as he joined the group. "The King does not heed him, it seems."

"No. But it does not stop that red-clad devil trying."

"He does the same with Parker." Susanna looked at Elizabeth's taut face.

"Aye, I'm sure he does." Elizabeth did not smile. "There is a rumor that Parker knows something that can bring him down. Perhaps that is why Wolsey hops from foot to foot like a bird on a branch. He wishes to get in first and turn the tale to his advantage."

Susanna went still. "What rumor is this?"

Elizabeth gave her a measured look. "Thomas Wyatt told my brother, my husband, and George Boleyn that Parker has information that could be the end of Wolsey."

No doubt that was why Thomas Boleyn had Parker cornered.

Susanna took a deep breath. "Did he mention what this information was?"

Elizabeth shook her head. "I hope it's true. Is it?"

Susanna did not answer. She moved toward Parker and he saw her coming, saw her face, and cut Boleyn off.

They met halfway.

"Wyatt—"

"I know."

"And Wolsey waits anxiously to speak to the King, even though the King ignores him. I think he's heard the rumor as well. I think he plans to lie, to cast another as the villain. Perhaps even you."

Parker nodded, his eyes narrowing. He strode forward and bowed deeply to the Queen. "Your Majesty." He bowed to the King, and then nodded to Wolsey.

Susanna followed behind him and curtsied deeply. The Queen looked at her, round and sharp-eyed as a bird, and Susanna's stomach sank. Those eyes looked as if she would pierce her through like a worm.

The Queen did not know her. They had never been introduced. Susanna repressed a sigh. Would her father ever have sent her here, if he had known that all thought her the King's mistress, simply because she was young and often seen leaving His Majesty's chambers?

Parker was occupied with the King and Wolsey, unable to introduce her to the Queen, and it was unthinkable that she introduce herself. She moved back to stand again at Elizabeth Carew's side, and turned to the tableau of king, courtier, and cardinal.

Wolsey seemed to stumble as her gaze clashed with his, and he had to jerk himself away to avoid jostling the King. Henry turned to him, his brow creased in annoyance.

"My pardon, Your Majesty." In the wrong, having almost toppled onto the King, Wolsey bowed low. When he lifted his head, his eyes were hot and bitter.

"Parker. That matter . . ." Henry swung away from the others and Parker moved to stand beside him, cutting Wolsey off.

"My lord, I have something to say that cannot wait." Wolsey's voice rang too loud in the confines of the gallery, and all conversation stopped.

The King turned. "And would you say it now, before all who stand with us?"

"I would prefer not." Wolsey gave a half bow, awaiting the King's pleasure.

Parker murmured something in the King's ear.

"Come, let us step a little away, then." Henry motioned with his hand, and Wolsey shot Parker a look of triumph. It faded immediately as Wolsey realized the King meant Parker to join them.

Susanna felt a touch on her arm.

"I never would have thought to see this confrontation with my own eyes." It was Francis Bryan, come to stand with her and his sister, and he dipped his head in a bow.

Susanna nodded, too distracted to curtsy. "I hope it is not a confrontation. I hope Parker can turn the talk to safe ground."

Bryan watched the trio with eyes hungry for blood, for the singing whisper of steel freshly drawn. "In that, my lady, in this whole gallery, you stand alone."

# 21

*A prince ought to have no other aim or thought, nor select anything else for his study, than war and its rules and discipline.*

—Machiavelli, The Prince, *chapter 14*

"You have news?" Henry inclined toward Wolsey, and Parker saw the flash of respect in the King's face. He needed always to remember that Wolsey lifted the massive burden of administrating England from the King's shoulders. The King had plenty to thank Wolsey for.

The Cardinal most definitely had the royal ear, and he would use that for all it was worth today.

"Disturbing information was given to me today. A diamond cutter I hired to revalue your jewels was found dead." Wolsey flicked a look at Parker, expecting some reaction.

Parker kept his face impassive. He had not realized Wolsey did not know of Jens's death. Perhaps the diamond cutter *had* been planning to run from Wolsey when he was cut down. Or perhaps Wolsey was merely using the diamond cutter's death now because it suited him.

"That is sad news, but I do not understand the urgency—"

"My pardon, Your Majesty. The matter is urgent because some days back, he mentioned there was a jewel not where it should be when he went through the inventory. He was endeavoring to find out where it was when he was killed."

Henry glanced at Parker, a flicker of worry, and Parker narrowed his eyes. It was a cunning counterattack.

"What jewel do you speak of?" The King crossed his arms over his chest. There was a sudden tension about him, the cords in his neck and hands standing out in relief.

"The Mirror of Naples, Your Majesty." Wolsey spoke the words so low, both Parker and the King had to lean forward to hear him.

"And did your man find where the jewel had gone?" The King's tension thickened around him, and his words came out clipped and hard.

Wolsey shook his head cautiously, like a deer in a hunter's sights. "He thought it must surely be mislaid, or away for cleaning. He was waiting for a reply from the Master of the King's Jewels when he was struck down. By a bolt." Wolsey let that sink in. "I think he was silenced."

Henry frowned. "Who do you suspect silenced him? If you think to accuse Sir Henry Wyatt, my Master of the Jewels has never picked up a weapon in all the years I've known him."

Wolsey opened his hands wide, palms out, the innocent messenger. "I suspect and accuse no one. I merely come to inform Your Majesty that your largest diamond is missing and the man trying to find it is dead."

"There you are wrong." Parker held Wolsey's gaze. "The man trying to find it is standing before you."

Wolsey was not quick enough. The surprise and fear on his face were visible to the King, and his hands trembled against his red robes as he realized it.

"Indeed." Henry turned to look out of the gallery to where the Fleet spilled into the Thames. "Parker came to me with this the day I returned to Bridewell, and has been looking into it."

"Then I am sure the matter is in good hands." Now all Wolsey wanted was to retreat. Retreat and find some new way to come at this.

Parker would not give him the chance if he were able.

"My Lord Chancellor, I have spoken with the Clerk of the King's Jewels on this matter and he claims no knowledge of the whereabouts of the Mirror. He also claims the last person to have access to the jewel was your diamond cutter, sent there at your express request and over the protests of his father."

Wolsey went very still. "He points a finger at me? *Me?*"

Parker shrugged. "No more than you point a finger at him."

"Enough." Henry turned back to the conversation. "The jewel must be found. If it truly is stolen, it must be recovered. And anyone who aided in its theft will be for the Tower."

Wolsey did not so much as flinch at that. Perhaps he thought no matter what, he would never be for the Tower. He had made himself too valuable to the King.

"And if it is the French? If they have taken it?" Despite his threat to the Comte, Parker had no wish to see England at war. He knew full well there wasn't the money for it.

"If the Mirror has been stolen, and if it is France, there is no choice but to war."

Wolsey turned his head sharply. "Your Majesty, even with the grant I am trying to collect, there will not be the funds—"

"Bah." Henry cut him off. "France's king is a prisoner, their army in ruins. If the Emperor will support us, we cannot fail."

Wolsey rubbed a hand on his forehead. "France is vast, and we have not the resources to equip . . ." His voice petered out, as if he'd already said this too many times.

Henry eyed the small feast. "I will not stand huddled in corners whispering all morning. Let us eat."

Wolsey bowed. "If Your Majesty will excuse me, I have matters that need my attention."

Henry lifted a hand to give him leave to go and Parker watched Wolsey hurry away.

By coming to the King with this, distancing himself from the Mirror and subtly pointing a finger of blame, the Cardinal had given himself away.

Either he still intended to give the jewel to the French, or he did not know where it was.

Either way, the Cardinal was a desperate man.

———

Harry was waiting for them when they stepped out into the courtyard at Bridewell. He leaned against the cart, chatting to Peter Jack, and Susanna could see from the way they stood together how they had once shared space under Old Swan dock as a place to sleep out of the rain.

There was an easy way to both of them now: they were less like mice and more like cats—their twitchiness had given way to focus. Peter Jack was far more dangerous now than he had been before, and Harry was more dangerous still. As he noticed her and Parker, he straightened and drew himself up.

"News?" Parker kept his voice low.

"Aye. This." Harry held out a roll of parchment, and Parker took it with a frown.

"A message? Who delivered it?"

"A Frenchman. Stopped me in the street."

Parker went still and Susanna's heart began a slow, hard thump. "They have been following you, then. How else did they know who you are?" Her voice was not as steady as she would have liked.

Harry nodded. Although he was trying to appear relaxed, his shoulders were stiff, his fingers curled too tight in on themselves. He would not like to think he'd been stalked, followed, without knowing it.

Parker broke the wax seal and Susanna watched his face.

"It is from the Comte." His attention was on the letter as he spoke, and when he lifted his gaze, Susanna saw deep worry in his eyes. "He wants to talk to me."

"*Nee.*" The word flew out of her mouth in Flemish without any bidding.

"I will do it on my own terms." Parker rolled the parchment as he stared off at the lane leading from the palace to Fleet Street.

He seemed to come back to himself. "Harry, call your boys."

Harry nodded, and Peter Jack rubbed his hands on his thighs in a gesture both nervous and eager.

Susanna put a hand on Parker's arm. "You could call on Francis Bryan." She looked back at the palace. "And any number of those you saved last month. They could help you, too."

He shook his head, helping her climb up into the cart with his uninjured arm, then swinging up beside her. Peter Jack scrambled to the back, and Harry pulled himself up as well.

"Parker." Her voice was sharp with worry.

"I could." He let Harry take the reins and the cart horse moved slowly forward. "But there will be strings attached to their help, no matter what I've done for them in the past. And I cannot say their hatred of Wolsey won't jeopardize things."

Susanna remembered Bryan's face as they'd stood together in the gallery. "They do hate him."

"Aye. Enough that they would plunge England into war to bring him down."

"What will you do?"

He grinned. "I will parley with the French."

# 22

*But a man is not often found sufficiently circumspect to*
*know how to accommodate himself to the change, both*
*because he cannot deviate from what nature inclines*
*him to do, and also because, having always prospered by*
*acting in one way, he cannot be persuaded that it is well*
*to leave it; and, therefore, the cautious man, when it is*
*time to turn adventurous, does not know how to do it,*
*hence he is ruined.*

—Machiavelli, The Prince, *chapter 25*

Parker watched the Comte's house from a small stand of trees, wondering if Susanna was right.

He could have called on any number of men to help him. But so often, the problems he dealt with could not become well-known. And none of those men, not even the best, were trustworthy with a bottle of wine down their gullet and a bit of music playing in the room.

If this didn't go to plan, if the Mirror had been stolen and there was no way to get it back—far, far better that no one knew of it, no one could talk of it, than that it become common knowledge.

With the sting of gossip lashing at him, the King would

not hesitate to go to war. As long as only a few knew of it and kept it that way, that possibility was lessended.

Norfolk and Wyatt were the problems.

Parker shifted his position, suddenly uncomfortable, as if there were eyes on him, and turned to look behind him. There was nothing but the dance of branches in the wind and the growing shadows of dusk. He turned his attention to the mansion again.

He'd been caught by surprise by Wyatt gossiping to the Boleyns and their circle. At least he hadn't told them everything. And at least Bryan and Carew were truly loyal to the King.

They would not say anything if he explained the stakes, but Thomas Boleyn . . . Boleyn was like a rat crouched under a kitchen cupboard, quivering with readiness for every morsel he could take for himself. He would use this to his greatest benefit, no matter the cost to others.

A light flickered to life in the hallway, shining through the small glasswork decoration above the door, and a tingle ran down Parker's back. The Comte was getting ready to leave.

He heard the sound of horse hooves, and as he had done the night before, a stable boy led two horses around the side of the house to the front steps.

One of the big double doors swung open and the Comte stepped out, a thick cloak about his shoulders.

Parker knew where he was going—he had named the place of the meeting himself—but he wanted to know who the Comte was bringing with him.

If he could still function, he suspected the assassin could, too.

The doors remained open while the Comte swung himself up into the saddle. He turned his head, sharp and impatient, and another figure stepped out.

There was a stiffness to him. He did not move with the fluid grace of before, but it was the same man. The man Parker had begun to think of as his nemesis.

The man pulled himself into the saddle with less agility and more care than the Comte had taken, and the light in the groom's hand glinted off the crossbow hanging from his belt.

The men moved off with quiet purpose, and Parker watched until they were out of the drive and disappeared down the street.

His horse was hidden down the road, with one of Harry's lads watching it. He needed to get to it, to move on to the meeting place where Harry and Peter Jack waited for him.

After a long hour crouched down, his whole focus on the mansion, his legs cramped as he stood. He stretched them, rolling his shoulders to relieve the ache across his neck. He winced as hot darts of pain shot down his right side. He rubbed around his wound with cautious fingers, blinking back the spots floating before his eyes.

He kept forgetting he was injured.

There was a sharp crack behind him as a twig snapped in two, and he spun around. A blow slammed into him just where his fingers had been moments before. White-hot agony engulfed him and he fell, scrabbling for handholds to consciousness.

The blow came again, vicious and purposeful, and he plummeted under, welcoming the drop to oblivion.

---

"**P**arker is missing!"

Harry burst through the back door into the kitchen, panic and fear on his face. He was gasping, hauling in breath.

Susanna's throat closed up and she clenched the table as she stood.

Mistress Greene and Eric rose with her as Peter Jack came in behind Harry, his chest heaving.

"Tell me."

"He was watching the Comte's house, to know if the assassin would accompany the Comte to the meeting. We had lads stationed along the way, to see if and when the assassin peeled off. Thought he might hide and try to take a shot at Parker."

"And?" She forced herself to sound steady and calm.

"The assassin came, but he stayed with the Comte. They are both still waiting at Queenhithe docks. Waiting for Parker."

"He didn't shoot Parker?" Susanna felt a sliver of hope.

Harry shook his head. "If he did, he did it at the house. But then why would they go to the meeting place? Why are they still waiting there?"

"Where could Parker have gone?" She frowned, tried to think through all the implications.

"Nowhere." Peter Jack threw his hands wide. "He was

going to wait and see who stepped out with the Comte, and then follow behind them."

Harry nodded. "If they got too far ahead, he could find out from my lads where the assassin had gone. Then the plan was for him to slip in behind the assassin and take him by surprise."

"Did he do that?"

"No." Peter Jack's voice was hoarse. "He never even followed them. He didn't even come for his horse."

There was a faint ringing in her ears now. Getting louder and louder, along with the thump of her heart. "Did you go to where he was watching the Comte's house?"

Harry nodded. His eyes slid away, and Susanna realized their panic wasn't at Parker's disappearance—it was at what they found where he'd been waiting. "Tell me, Harry."

"Blood." He whispered the word. "There was a struggle, from the markings on the ground. And there was blood."

"They may still want you, my lady," Eric said from beside the fire. "Maybe they waited to keep up a pretense. So they could follow Harry and Peter Jack straight back here."

# 23

*Hence it is to be remarked that, in seizing a state, the usurper ought to examine closely into all those injuries which it is necessary for him to inflict, and to do them all at one stroke so as not to have to repeat them daily; and thus by not unsettling men he will be able to reassure them, and win them to himself by benefits.*

—Machiavelli, The Prince, *chapter 8*

Parker came to hard and fast, aware of the cold, the pain, and the dark in an instant. He kept still, trying to absorb a sense of the place.

He lay on stone. The chill had seeped through his clothes, into his bones, and numbed his skin. The hardness left him feeling bruised and stiff.

He was alone. He guessed it from the air, which was stale, musty, with a strange sour-sweet odor. As he breathed it in it clung to his face, damp and freezing, invading his throat and lungs and taking up residence with bat claws.

The darkness was as solid as the stones he lay on.

A crypt, perhaps. Or a cellar. From the smell, he had a sinking feeling it was a crypt.

His shoulder throbbed and burned, and he gently felt around his wound. Felt the hard stiffness of dried blood on his sleeve and his chest, and then the sticky wetness where the wound still seeped blood.

He was shivering, and every tiny shake of his body slammed another nail into his shoulder. He sensed he'd been thrown to lie where he fell on the floor, and, like an old man, cramped and aching, he forced his feet under him and stood.

The knife was gone from his sleeve, and he slid a hand into his boot. Nothing.

His sword was also missing.

He swayed, disoriented and adrift.

He was defenseless.

And then, somewhere high above, he heard bells ringing.

---

"They're gone," one of Harry's lads called before they'd even opened the kitchen door to his wild rapping.

He tumbled into the room, looking exactly like a merchant's page, a look cultivated to render the boy invisible. Parker had suggested the outfits and provided them, and had reaped tenfold on his investment.

"The Comte and his man?" Harry stood.

"Aye. The traffic at Queenhithe was getting thinner and thinner as the evening wore on, and they eventually gave up. I followed them back to the Comte's house." He sank into a chair, stretching his hands toward the fire.

Mistress Greene served him some stew. "Well, if they went home, they weren't following anyone."

"I need to speak to them," Susanna said. "If they are home now, I can go straight there."

Peter Jack stared at her. "They will kill you."

Susanna lifted her shoulders. "If they really want to kill me, then they will. Unless I'm willing to be a prisoner in this house, they will get enough chances. And every moment we delay is another Parker is missing."

Harry nodded, the movement slow and considering. "Why don't I go with another note, first? Set up another meeting. Their reaction to that will tell me a lot more about whether they have Parker than they'd tell me willingly."

Susanna rocked on her feet, undecided. "I don't want to waste time."

"It's a good compromise, my lady." Mistress Greene's hands were clasped before her. "You don't want to throw yourself at them in sacrifice if there is another way."

Susanna nodded and turned to Harry. "You can approach them first, and take Peter Jack with you. I'll come too and wait somewhere safe. That way we can proceed to the meeting if they agree, or come home."

Harry nodded, looking relieved. "What will you say in the note?"

Susanna tapped her fingers. "Where would be a good place to meet them for a second time?"

"St. Mary Woolnoth." Peter Jack glanced at Harry, who nodded in accord.

"That's close enough to the Comte's house that he will be more inclined to meet a second time, yet far enough from us that they won't easily follow us back without being seen," he said.

"We meet outside the church?" Susanna looked to Peter Jack and he nodded. "Then I'll write the note."

"What else will you say?" Harry watched her, his eyes dark and worried.

She sighed. "That Parker has gone missing, and I need to speak to them. If they have taken Parker, I won't be telling them anything they don't already know. If they haven't, it should get their attention."

"If they haven't taken him, we have no use for them. They may still want to silence you, and be pleased someone else has taken care of Parker for them," Harry said bluntly.

Susanna squared her shoulders. "I'm not that easy to kill."

———

The churchyard was well kept. Susanna could see hardly at all in the darkness, but the damp grass she knelt on at the back of the building was short and lush.

Harry had offered to leave the lamp for her, but she knew they would need it, and it would look strange for them to arrive without one.

She thought of Parker, of where he could be, and of the blood Harry had found where he'd been taken. Helpless panic battered her from within, like a bird trapped in a chimney, and she sat back against the wall and hugged her knees to her chest, rocking herself for comfort.

The Comte must be responsible.

If he wasn't . . . She did not know where she would start. Parker had more than his share of enemies, but he had plenty of friends, too. Including the King himself.

There was nowhere she wouldn't go, no one she wouldn't speak to, to find out where Parker could be.

A gate creaked on its hinges to her right, the way she had come into the yard from the front of the church, and she was glad she was sitting down in deep shadow.

Whoever entered had no light.

She held still, straining to hear where they were.

There should be noise, the sound of footsteps or a voice. The utter silence told her someone stood within the court-yard, listening just as intently as she did.

There was a quick, sharp rustle of clothing, and she felt the vibration of steps on the ground. They were moving away, walking down the yard toward the tree-lined far wall.

She stood, pressing up against the cold stone of the church, then began moving quietly toward the gate.

The church wall was comfortingly solid beneath her hands, and before she moved along the fence toward the gate, she kept still and listened again.

There was no sound at all. The wind had died, and not even the trees rustled. Her skin pricked and fear sank its teeth into her neck, forcing a shiver from her.

She took a step toward the gate and a figure rose up from the ground right at her feet, arms outstretched.

She screamed, the sound bouncing against the church and

then swallowed by the night as she was knocked to the ground with a hand clamped over her mouth.

She looked up at a face so shadowed she could not make out the features, and saw a crossbow aimed in line with her chest.

"Madame, do not move. I failed to shoot you at London Bridge, but I promise you, I will not fail again."

# 24

Susanna reared up despite the bolt aimed at her heart.
"What have you done with the boys?"

The assassin swore and lowered the bow. "They are un-
harmed. They sit waiting for the Comte in his hallway. They
think he is being roused from his chamber."

Relief buckled her knees and she fell back to the ground, a
hand to her throat. "Good. That's good."

"What is this about, madame? You waste our time all evening, then ask for a second meeting, but do not come to the
door yourself. Your man plays dangerous games with you and
those boys—although what advantage he thinks this will
bring him, I do not know."

"He is missing." Susanna managed to get up on her knees. She knew she looked like a supplicant and that was what she was. "Someone took him just outside the Comte's house. We thought it might be you."

"I don't take prisoners." He lowered the bow further. "I only kill."

"Then where is he?" Susanna could hear her voice fraying, and took a deep breath. "Where *is* he?"

"What was he doing at the Comte's house when he was taken?"

"Watching to see if you followed after the Comte. If you had plans to kill him at the meeting." She could not see his eyes, but she kept her gaze on his face.

"Ah. That was perhaps wise of him. But no. After last night, we thought it best to speak with him, face-to-face. To stop the games."

"I have to find him." Susanna rocked back to get her feet beneath her, and his hand came out to help her up. She took it, her hand closing over hard, calloused skin. He pulled her up easily, and she could feel his strength.

"Whoever took your courtier either knows he is interested in the Comte and they were waiting for him, or they followed him." His voice was deep, pleasant, and she still had not seen his face.

"Yes." Susanna realized he was as tall as Parker, but more wiry in build. "But Parker is not easy to follow."

"No, I would think not. So, someone who knows of his in-

terest in the Comte. That leaves a small list. We have managed to keep things very quiet."

"The Cardinal, and perhaps Norfolk." Two of the most
dangerous men in England.

"I thought it was just the Cardinal and his men. You think
the Duke of Norfolk knows, as well?"

Susanna lifted her shoulders, struck by the strangeness of
the conversation. "He knows something of what is happening.
He knew about the cloth merchant you were trying to kill yesterday. And about Jens. Whether he knows about the Comte,
I'm not sure." She was glad to be reminded he had killed Jens,
that he was not to be trusted.

"Your husband is working for the King?"

Susanna nodded. "He is."

"The Cardinal would not like that, I think. Wolsey is already in enough trouble with us. To have the King take notice
as well . . . He is the most likely suspect. I would approach him
first."

Susanna thought of the likelihood of Wolsey telling her
anything, and despair pulled her down. "Why are you helping
me? If there had not been so many people on the riverbank
yesterday, if Parker hadn't run straight for you, you would have
killed me and the cloth merchant."

He laughed with genuine humor. "Someone stopped
paying me to kill you as of this morning."

"Why was that?"

"Your husband found me and wounded me. Then my spy

saw him go straight to the King the next day." There was admiration in his voice. "It is clearly useless to kill him to stop him talking, as he has already talked. When a thing is unnecessary, the money for it dries up."

"He is not my husband," Susanna said quietly. "He is my betrothed, and I want him back."

"I could offer you aid." The assassin spoke in a matter-of-fact voice, shifting the bow so it leaned on his leg. "I am quite willing, in exchange for something I want."

Surprised, she kept her voice as steady as she could. "And what would that be?"

He shifted again in the dark. "The Mirror of Naples, of course."

———————

Harry and Peter Jack looked sick as she came through the Comte's front door, the assassin behind her.

He wore his brown cloak again, unmistakably the man from the bank of the Thames. Harry rose up and Susanna felt the assassin's quick movement behind her. She turned and saw the crossbow aimed over her shoulder, directly at Harry.

"Sit, Harry. He means me no harm."

Peter Jack opened his mouth and she cut him off with her hand. "Apparently I am more useful alive now than dead."

"Indeed." There was something in the assassin's voice, chagrin, perhaps.

She turned to get her first clear look at him, and he returned her look and gave a bow. "Enchanté, madame."

He was dark and elegant, his eyes almost black, and his skin looked sun touched, though it surely could not have seen a sunny day for many months.

She dipped her head and her knees in a curtsy. There was a sound from the staircase, a creak of wood, and she turned and locked gazes with the Comte, who was on the last step. He was beautifully dressed, as if about to go out.

"Madame." His gaze brushed over her and then locked on the assassin. "What have we here, Jean?"

"We may have a new way forward." Jean shrugged casually, as if this was not really his concern and he merely provided an alternative.

"And that would be?"

"Mistress Horenbout has some insight into this affair, and access to people and places we do not. She may be willing to assist us."

"And what does the good mistress require in exchange?" The Comte's eyes were on her now with real interest.

"She needs help in finding her betrothed."

"Her betrothed . . ." The Comte frowned. "The King's man? He is missing?"

"Missing and injured."

"And who says he wasn't taken and harmed by you?" Harry stood, feet braced apart, and glared at Jean.

"Because, as I told your mistress, I do not take prisoners. I only kill."

"You wouldn't have wanted the body lying near this house, though, would you? The sheriff would've been called round, and I don't think that would suit you. You could have dumped him anywhere." Peter Jack stood as well.

Susanna hadn't thought of that possibility, and she turned sharply to Jean. "Is that what you've done?" How could she not have thought of this?

A wave of nausea washed over her, bathing her in cold, clammy sweat, and she leaned forward, her hands on her knees. "Let's go." She stood, breathing in deeply, as she spoke to the boys.

"What about our mutual promise of aid?" Jean blocked the way to the door.

Susanna stared at him. "I need a little time to work out the consequences. You must know the price you ask for your help is very high. High enough to land me on the headman's block."

"Your servants have made you distrust me." He flicked a look at Harry and Peter Jack that made her shiver.

"Monsieur, yesterday you tried to kill me and another man in front of my eyes. A few days earlier, you killed one of my father's oldest friends." She pointed a finger at his chest. "Less than a day ago you stabbed my betrothed with a jagged glass bottle, and now you wish me to believe you will help me find him and deliver him safely. And the price for your help is a jewel the sovereigns of two countries would go to war for."

She gathered her skirts about her and drew herself tall. "I do not need anyone to point out that I would be foolish to trust you blindly. Very foolish indeed."

He said nothing for a moment, then stepped aside. "And you are anything but foolish, madame."

As she went past him, he reached out and grabbed her shoulder and she jerked to a halt.

He bent down and spoke in her ear. "You know where to find me when you decide you need my help. You may not want to be foolish, but do not be too clever, either."

# 25

*Yet it cannot be called talent to slay fellow-citizens, to deceive friends, to be without faith, without mercy, without religion; such methods may gain empire, but not glory.*

—*Machiavelli*, The Prince, *chapter 8*

They walked home in silence.

Harry had begun to speak just outside the Comte's door, but Susanna had shaken her head, and neither he nor Peter Jack had opened their mouths again.

She could tell they were looking for the Comte's spies along the road, but she didn't bother. She spent every step thinking through her choices, laying out the pieces of the puzzle just as she would lay out her pigments and brushes before she went to work.

When she climbed the stairs to the back door and stepped into the kitchen, panic and desperation had loosened their hold a little.

"How many did you see?" Harry spoke to Peter Jack as they closed the door behind her.

"Three."

"I did, too, but I wager there were more."

Susanna lifted off her cloak and hung it on a hook near the door. "They must have seen me slip into the churchyard and sent word to the Comte. Jean knew exactly where to find me."

"And there we sat, like two fat lumps, waiting in the Comte's hall," Harry said with disgust.

"It doesn't matter. He did me no harm, and we have information we did not have before, as well as an offer of help." Susanna slid into a chair, her voice soft so as not to wake Mistress Greene and Eric.

"You won't accept it, will you?" Harry joined her, getting close to the fire. He shivered as the warmth reached him, and rubbed his hands together.

"I may have no choice." She rubbed stiff fingers under her cap. "I cannot go to Norfolk. I do not trust him and he would not willingly help Parker. The other men that come to mind . . ." She thought of Francis Bryan, of Guildford and Courtenay. All men who owed Parker their lives. But would they act with the urgency needed?

"You could speak with Simon." Peter Jack had not sat, his cloak still around him. "I can fetch him now."

Susanna nodded, but as he turned to go, a thought struck her. "Wait. Say nothing of the bargain Jean has offered. If I'm forced to take it, I would rather no one knows of it."

"But surely Jean is taking a gamble? He has not been able to find the jewel himself; why does he think you could get it?"

"He doesn't strike me as a man who would gamble with something this big." She twined her fingers round and round, round and round . . . then froze. Why hadn't she seen it before? "He knows where the jewel is." Certainty struck deeper with every word. "He just cannot get to it."

"And he thinks you can?" Harry's eyes narrowed.

"It must be hidden in the palace, or somewhere else I have access. Somewhere no one would question my presence."

"I think you're right." Peter Jack dropped his hand from the door handle. "Which means if he can find Parker, can bring him to us . . ."

A heavy, roiling serpent took up residence in her stomach. "I would be obliged to commit treason."

———

B ridewell was lit with candles and lanterns. As she walked down the passageways, she thought there was an extra gleam on everything tonight, as if there were some special occasion.

She had chosen not to involve Simon.

If things didn't work out, if she ended her days on the headman's block, she wanted her taint on as few people as possible. That Harry and Peter Jack were already deep in the mire hung heavily on her, but as Parker's servants, they would be suspect anyway. There was no shielding them.

If there was no other solution, she would follow in the steps of the King's sister, Queen Mary. She would give the jewel in exchange for her lover's life.

She hoped there was a better way.

She reached the antechamber to the Privy Chamber and realized with dread that she'd arrived at a bad time.

The King was not dining quietly in his rooms tonight, nor with the Queen. He was entertaining.

There was music, and Susanna saw that the flute player she knew from Ghent was still in the King's service. As usual, he acknowledged her entrance with a high, sweet trill, lifting the flute up and tipping back his head.

The small display of friendship and solidarity from a fellow countryman helped. She breathed in and began to look for the King.

She heard the murmur of French and German, of her native Flemish and Dutch, as she slipped between the beautifully dressed men and women. There were wealthy merchants here tonight, as well as clergymen and nobles from the principalities of Europe.

Her heart sank.

This was not the time and place to speak with the King, but now was all she had. The thought of postponing her audience made her sick.

She could not wait.

"It is strange to see you about, my lady, without Parker scowling like a fierce hawk at your shoulder." The words were spoken lightly, with humor, and a hand touched her arm.

Susanna turned, and at the sight of Will Somers her panic lifted a little. The Fool was dressed all in black tonight, and her image of him as a quick-witted and humorous Death was made all the stronger.

She opened her mouth and then closed it again. Somers may be kind and .wish her well, but anything she said was fair game to the King's fool. There would be no keeping Parker's disappearance a secret if he knew of it.

She frowned, weighing the benefits and drawbacks of Parker's disappearance remaining a secret.

"I think you have decided the fate of mankind and put to rest the secrets of alchemy in these few short moments, my lady. Never have I seen a brain working so fast."

"My pardon." Susanna lowered her eyes and hoped she looked suitably demure. But when she lifted her head, Will Somers was watching her, his head tilted to the side.

"What is afoot, my lady?"

She shook her head, a twinge of regret in the movement. There was something about Somers that made her want to trust him, but not enough to risk Parker.

"I need to speak with the King, and did not realize he would be occupied this evening."

A laugh rolled out from the center of the room, and Susanna stilled. The King was surrounded by men in fine velvet doublets, all taking care not to crowd him too much.

Susanna set her shoulders back and started forward. With

one long stride, Somers grabbed her shoulder and held her back.

"You'll do more harm than good to approach him tonight. He is in a vicious mood. There is no news yet from the Emperor on a war with France, and he is impatient to move ahead."

The King laughed again, and Susanna raised an eyebrow at Somers.

"He laughs, but darkness lies no deeper than the scratch of a fingernail beneath the surface. Before the dinner began, he sent Wolsey scurrying away when he tried to come forward with another complaint about Parker. It is the first time I've seen the King lose his temper with the Cardinal."

Susanna gripped Somers's long black sleeve. "What did Wolsey say about Parker?"

Somers shrugged. "Barely anything before the King went red in the face. A line about Parker conspiring with the French."

Rage flashed through Susanna like a lightning strike. Every sense was alive and burning, her body ready for battle. If Wolsey had been nearby, she would have thrown the knife that was up her sleeve straight for his eye.

Somers stepped back. "You are no friend of the Cardinal tonight either, I see." For the first time, there was a hint of uncertainty in his eyes.

She drew in her breath between clenched teeth. "I am no friend of his ever."

She turned. If Somers was right, she would not approach

the King tonight. But now she knew where she could go. Wolsey's complaints held the smack of preparation, of setting up Parker as a scapegoat.

And scapegoats were kept tethered to a pole, safely chained as they awaited their fate.

"Where are you going, my lady?" Somers's soft call made her look over her shoulder.

"To find a pole."

# 26

*A wise prince ought to observe some such rules, and never in peaceful times stand idle, but increase his resources with industry in such a way that they may be available to him in adversity, so that if fortune chances it may find him prepared to resist her blows.*

—Machiavelli, The Prince, *chapter 14*

Before she reached the door, a hand fell on her shoulder in a strong grip. A tight-knit group of Frenchmen closed in around her, shielding her from the rest of the room.

Susanna glared at the man holding her. She was tired of being manhandled. "You move quickly, Monsieur le Comte." She tugged and he released her with a little dip of his head.

"No faster than you, madame. You wasted no time coming to the King." The men around them were pretending not to listen, and he took her arm again to steer her to a little alcove in a private corner.

"I know you have heard of the argument between Wolsey and the King. In fact, I know to the precise moment when you did hear it. I saw your face," he said.

"That must have been a blow to your plans." She had damped down the rage she felt at Wolsey, but now it came roaring back to life. "Did you think somehow Wolsey's accusations wouldn't reach my ears?"

"We are not behind this." The Comte slammed his fist into his open palm. "Madame, on my life, we did not lie to you tonight. We do not know where your betrothed is."

"Then you must at least be pleased with what has happened tonight. Wolsey intends to give you the jewel, if he's trying to lay blame on Parker in advance. Otherwise all he needs do is to return the jewel to its place."

The Comte started, suddenly alert. "You do not know. Wolsey has told us very clearly he will not give us the Mirror of Naples."

"Why not?"

"Because he does not know where it is."

Susanna did not move. "How can that be?"

The Comte shrugged. "Because Jens of Antwerp panicked. That is the only explanation. I don't think Wolsey told him exactly what he would be doing when he got to London."

"And when he realized what it really was, he went a little . . . mad." That would explain a great deal.

The Comte nodded. "When Jens fell out with Wolsey, the Cardinal denied him access to the palace. That is when Jens began running around London, approaching friends for a way out of the country."

"Jean killed him." She wanted to wash her skin where the

Comte had touched her; there was too much blood on his hands.

The Comte looked down his aquiline nose at her. "I understand your distrust of us. But we are willing to help you get what you want, if you help us get what we want."

"You ask a great deal."

He shrugged. "I have no choice. And you have no betrothed."

"You know where the Mirror is? You seem so sure I can get it for you."

"I have a good idea."

"But you do not know where Parker is. Why shouldn't I simply look without you?"

"Because Wolsey is a powerful man, and if he wants your betrothed hidden, hidden he will be. I have spies all through this city, men who hear many things. We have a better chance of finding him than you do."

Susanna took a step back. "I will think on it a little longer. The stakes are very high to gamble on the strength of your guess."

"Certainly." The Comte gave a stiff bow; frustration and impatience shimmered off him with every jerky movement.

She dipped a curtsy and slipped through the crowd to the door.

Just as she stepped out, she felt the weight of a gaze on her and turned.

Norfolk stood in the middle of the room, watching her. The look in his eyes was not comforting.

---

The door swung shut behind her, and Susanna resisted the urge to lean back against it in relief to be out of the room.

She stepped forward, and found her way blocked by a young woman. She looked exotic, with a slight tilt to her dark eyes and thick, dark hair. She clasped her hands nervously before her.

Susanna remembered her face from the time she'd spent in the Queen's chambers more than a month ago.

"My lady. The Queen wishes an audience."

Susanna's heart squeezed painfully in her chest. She already suspected the Queen had no love for her, and she would have even less if Susanna refused a direct summons.

"I am honored, my lady. But I have an urgent matter—"

"Please." The woman's eyes darted left and right, and she stepped closer, placed a hand on Susanna's arm. "I am Gertrude Courtenay, Henry Courtenay's wife." She drew Susanna across to the shadows on the other side of the passageway.

A flicker of surprise went through Susanna. Henry Courtenay was one of the four men she and Parker had saved from being named as conspirators against the Crown in February.

"I know what my husband and I owe you. I am one of the Queen's favorites. My mother is Spanish and my father is the Queen's chamberlain. My aunt is one of the Queen's closest friends. She came over to England with the Queen when she was first married to the King's brother. I have some influence and I will use it to your benefit, but please, come."

"I thank you for that." Susanna hesitated, then took a small risk. "I truly would be honored to attend the Queen, but I find myself in a situation as bad as your husband was in last month. If I do not hurry, the ending will not be so happy for me."

Gertrude stiffened, and her fingers dug in to Susanna's arm. "I see. May I ask if there is any help I can give you in this?"

Susanna shook her head.

"Does this involve the Cardinal Wolsey?"

Susanna grabbed her, held her close. "Why do you ask that?"

"Because it is all over the court that not an hour ago, the King and Wolsey exchanged heated words over your betrothed. Usually the Cardinal only comes to court on Sundays, but since the King's mishap in the country, he has remained at Bridewell. That in itself is worthy of note. But never before has the King lost his temper with Wolsey so openly."

Susanna nodded. "Wolsey is involved."

"Then you should come with me. But say nothing of this in the general hearing of the ladies. The Cardinal has spies among the women."

Susanna resisted Gertrude's tug on her sleeve. "Are you sure this will help me more than confronting Wolsey directly?"

Gertrude laughed without any trace of mirth. "Unless you have a weapon to hand, yes."

Susanna stared at her, not looking away, and Gertrude cleared her throat. "Even if you have a weapon, my way will surely be the better one, I swear. I mean to repay the debt I have to you for my husband's life, and for the well-being of my family. I have a way for you to get the better of the Cardinal."

Susanna allowed herself to be pulled down the passage, away from the Cardinal's rooms.

She only hoped it was the right way to go.

# 27

*When princes have thought more of ease than of arms
they have lost their states.*

—Machiavelli, The Prince, *chapter 14*

The Queen's chambers were less sumptuous than the King's, but Susanna knew it was from the Queen's preference, rather than any lack of funds from her husband.

The antechamber was not so full as the last time Susanna had entered it, and she assumed many of the ladies were below at the reception, attending their husbands or fathers.

As soon as she stepped into the chamber, Gertrude's manner became cooler, more distant. "Please wait a moment while I see if the Queen will receive you now."

Susanna curtsied low. She did not doubt Wolsey had spies here. Norfolk must have some, too, although he preferred servants rather than nobility to act as his eyes and ears. They could be paid with money, rather than favors.

Gertrude slipped into the Queen's chamber and Susanna kept her eyes on the door, her hands clenched as tight as her stomach.

"Mistress Horenbout."

The woman who approached her looked sharp and hard. She wore fine clothes, but there was a musty smell of sweat about her. Susanna did not recognize her from her last visit to the Queen's chambers.

"'Tis late for the Queen to need the services of the King's painter." Her words were bright and brittle.

"How lucky, then, that I was in attendance." Susanna smiled, sweet as a lemon tart. "You have the better of me, my lady. You know my name, but I do not know yours."

"I am Jane Stafford. I have heard much about you, my lady. And I am curious, what commission has the Queen for you? I look forward to seeing it."

"A portrait of the Princess Mary," Susanna lied. "So when the princess is away from court, in the good air of the country, the Queen may look on it and be comforted."

"How delightful." Jane's words seemed to stick in her throat, thick and choking. It seemed she believed Susanna's lie.

She had clearly been hoping for something else. Something she could take back to Norfolk or Wolsey—whoever's pay she was in.

"The Queen will see you now." Gertrude stood in the doorway, the door open just enough to let her through, as if shielding the occupants of the room from view. Her gaze went to Jane Stafford and her lips pursed in a thin line.

"My lady." Susanna dipped her head in farewell and walked toward Gertrude.

"What did she want?" Gertrude whispered as she stood back to let Susanna enter.

"To know why I was here."

Gertrude shot another look at Jane, but she had turned away and was talking with a small group of women. Gertrude pulled the door closed, shutting them out. "What did you tell her?"

"I said the Queen has commissioned me to paint a small picture of the Princess to keep beside her and give her comfort while the Princess is away."

"That is a good idea."

Susanna looked up, surprised, to see the Queen and one other woman only in the large chamber. They were seated by a fire and it was the Queen who had spoken.

"Your Majesty." She curtsied low.

"Despite what we are really discussing here, Mistress Horenbout, I find the idea of a small painting of my daughter most delightful. You will paint it."

"Of course." Susanna curtsied low again.

"Now, what has the Cardinal put his meddling fingers into this time?"

---

The Queen was short, her shoulders round and plump. The woman with her was beautiful, a Spanish lady from the parting in her dark hair, to the tips of her wide, pink-lined sleeves.

"This is my aunt, Maria." Gertrude went to stand beside her aunt's chair, and Susanna could see the resemblance. "She is visiting the Queen for a few weeks."

Susanna curtsied again. "My lady."

It was clear these three were a close-knit group. Susanna felt fortunate to be owed a favor by Gertrude Courtenay; there was no question she was being privileged with this audience.

"I wanted to warn you tonight that Wolsey seems determined to cast John Parker in the worst possible light, but Gertrude tells me you are aware of it." Katherine watched her with eyes filled with intelligence.

"I think Wolsey has done worse than try to tarnish Parker's name, Your Majesty. I believe he has injured him and taken him somewhere. That somewhere, he is locked in a room, if he has not already been . . ." Susanna stopped, appalled at the way her voice was thickening, the way her breath was rasping in her throat. Her eyes seemed determined to shed the tears she had forbidden them to shed.

She closed them, tipped her head up, and forced herself to breathe deep. "My pardon."

"There have been many times I have felt just as you do now." Katherine's voice was low, and Susanna could hear a depth to it, of sorrow and of steel. "Wolsey even now plots to push my daughter aside and raise up my husband's bastard son in her place. There is very little I believe he would not do, and if it suited him to falsely accuse Parker, to keep him out of the way while he lays his traps, I have no doubt that is what he would do."

"I need to know what *I* can do." Tears leaked from the corners of Susanna's eyes and she rubbed them away with the backs of her hands. "I had thought to confront him—"

"Bah." Katherine chopped the air with a sharp hand. "That will accomplish nothing more than alerting him to what you know. There are other ways."

Susanna wanted to believe her. If it was possible to save Parker without relying on the Comte and Jean, that would be the best possible outcome.

"I used to have women spies in his household." Katherine watched her as she spoke, and Susanna realized the Queen must have told very few people that she had spies at all. She gave a little nod, to indicate approval and that she was ready to hear more.

"They have all been dismissed. Someone in my chambers either heard me talking of them, or read my private accounts and found the entries of their payment. But before they were sent away, I did learn something that may be of interest to you."

Susanna's heart gave a little skip.

"When Wolsey wants someone out of the way, someone whose actions or comments are inconvenient or who poses a threat to him, he has them sent to Fleet Prison. Many nobles have been sent to the Fleet by the Star Chamber or another court, but Wolsey has taken to sending people there with no due process whatsoever."

"How do those people get out?" Susanna clenched her hands to stop them trembling.

"When Wolsey has manufactured enough evidence against

them he makes their stay more official, or if they are no longer a threat, he releases them."

"Parker will never cease to be a threat to the Cardinal." She felt as if she were standing in some high place, where her words were snatched from her mouth as she uttered them.

"Indeed." The look Katherine gave her was pitying.

"There is a way into the Fleet that is not through the front gates." Gertrude stepped away from her aunt and reached for Susanna's hand. "The Queen's spies discovered Wolsey uses a tunnel from St. Sepulchre's Church to sneak the prisoners in. So there is no official record of them being admitted."

The Queen leaned forward, intense. "My spies in Wolsey's house heard about it one day in the kitchens. Wolsey employs two men to grab his enemies and drag them blindfolded to the Fleet through the tunnels. That way no one can report where they were held or point a finger back at him if he decides to release them."

"There is another tunnel between St. Sepulchre's and Newgate Prison." Gertrude released her hand, and Susanna felt the loss of warmth. "The priests use it to walk to Newgate and ring their Execution Bell at midnight on the day someone is to be condemned to death."

"But the passage to the Fleet is not generally known?"

The Queen leaned back in her chair, her hands gripping the arms. "We cannot say. It is impossible for any of us to go there without Wolsey knowing of it, and perhaps guessing our purpose. But my spies think this is a secret passage. It passes under St. George's Inn and comes out in the dungeons of the Fleet, they heard the Cardinal's men say."

"And you think that is where Parker is being kept?"

"If Wolsey were staying at Hampton Court, as is usual, I would say look there. But he has remained very close to the King since his return to Bridewell. He would not want Parker to be too far from him."

"Then I need to find this passage and see if Parker is indeed in the Fleet."

Katherine's expression was tense. "I urge you, first ask at the prison gate, or find someone to speak with a warden. If Parker is officially a prisoner, Wolsey has much against him. If not, then Wolsey is still gathering his lies."

Susanna nodded, and curtsied deeply. "Your Majesty, I thank you."

"Parker has given me aid before. And he is the one courtier of my husband's I can trust to always speak true. I will not stand by and let Wolsey bring him down."

Susanna dipped her head gratefully to Gertrude and her aunt, and turned to the door.

If Parker was in the Fleet, she would do anything to get him out. Even walk through the bowels of London itself.

# 28

*But to exercise the intellect the prince should read histo-*
*ries, and study there the actions of illustrious men, to*
*see how they have borne themselves in war, to examine*
*the causes of their victories and defeat, so as to avoid the*
*latter and imitate the former.*

—Machiavelli, The Prince, *chapter 24*

Fleet Prison loomed ominous and grim in the dark. A bell tolled—St. Sepulchre's. It was coming to matins, and she had not yet slept.

Harry and Peter Jack accompanied her, trudging along Ludgate Hill and up Fleet Lane without a word.

The Fleet River ran to her left, a constant hiss of sound that was suddenly drowned out by a cry from beyond the prison walls. It seemed to come from a dark, desolate place in the crier's soul, and raised the hair on the back of her neck. It cut off suddenly. And while she'd wanted badly for it to stop, now that it had, the silence was worse.

"Thanks to God that wailing has stopped," Harry muttered.

"No one about, this time of night." Peter Jack shivered

against the deep cold that rose from the river like fog, sneaking under cloaks and numbing faces and ears.

Susanna hugged herself and looked again at the massive, closed gates. "Perhaps there is a watchman. There must be." She pounded on the wood. "Hello?"

They listened in silence, and after long moments Susanna heard the scrape of boots on the other side of the gate.

A small panel slid open and a face appeared, ghostly white against the darkness. "Aye?"

Susanna swallowed. "Please, sir." Her voice trembled and for once she did not try to get it under control. She lifted a hand to her eyes. The tears suddenly glistening there were not false, but where she would usually have struggled not to show them, now she let them fall freely.

"Well?"

"I come to ask if my betrothed is here, sir. I heard a rumor—" She felt a sob rising up through her throat, tearing through her, and she choked it back. "I heard a rumor he has been sent here, but I am not certain."

"You want to know now?" The watchman spoke with an edge. There was a calculation to his outrage, and the way he waited for a response, she could almost imagine him rubbing his hands together.

"Yes, please, sir. I will most certainly pay you for your trouble." She spoke the required response with as much sincerity as she could muster. Harry and Peter Jack stood tense beside her, their eyes on the watchman, and she was never so grateful to have company in her life.

"Maybe I could ask the wardens—depending when he came in. Would it have been this morning?"

"No. Earlier this evening."

He lifted a hand to his chin, and his fingers rasped across it. "The wardens on duty will know if he's here, then. What is the name?"

"Parker." She took a deep breath. "John Parker."

He disappeared without a word, sliding the window closed with a snap.

Susanna only realized she was rocking back and forth when Peter Jack put a hand on her arm to stop her. His face was white, panicked, and she stood tall, letting her arms fall to her sides.

She wasn't the only one suffering.

"What if he isn't here?" Harry spoke very low.

"It will be bad enough if he is." Peter Jack shivered again. "This place is a fortress."

Susanna said nothing. There was almost no good answer. But if she knew he was here, at least she would know he was alive.

They heard the shuffle of footsteps, and Susanna spun to the gate, her fingernails digging into her palms.

The sliding window opened and the watchman's face appeared. He said nothing, and at last she realized he was waiting for payment.

She dug into her belt purse and pulled out three coins. His face disappeared, replaced quickly by an outstretched hand, and she dropped the money onto his palm.

She heard him counting it, making sure he thought it fair.

His face appeared again. "No John Parker come in this evening. Not above, nor down in Bartholomew Fair."

"What is Bartholomew Fair?" she whispered.

"Our less pleasant accommodation, in the cellars and dungeons." He cackled. "Men down there don't last long. Tend to die of jail fever."

"And he wasn't brought in?"

The watchman shook his head. "If he's here, he's in a cell without paying his lodging fee, or any other fee. Which is impossible." His little snigger turned into a hacking cough.

She nodded, and he closed the sliding window with a snap. She could hear him just the other side of the gate, shuffling his feet as he ambled away.

"I can't help being relieved." Peter Jack looked at the gates, massive enough to withstand the centuries.

The gate creaked, possibly with the wind, and Susanna also heard the tiny scrape of a shoe. As if someone leaned against the gate listening.

"Let's go home." She let defeat and despair fill her voice, and her steps away were heavy.

Parker *was* in there; she was certain of it. Shut away, hidden even from the wardens. Wolsey had not manufactured enough evidence against him yet.

Which left a problem.

If the wardens didn't know he was there, how would she find him?

---

A driving, relentless rain drummed into the ground. Susanna stood on the back step and watched the way it churned up splashes of mud with every hard drop.

"Take an extra cloak." Mistress Greene came from behind and pressed the thick wool into her hands.

Susanna's fingers clenched the fabric tight. It was an old cloak of Parker's, his scent still on it. She swirled it about her shoulders and felt immediately warmer, more focused.

"Your face is as white as a ghost." Mistress Greene handed her another mug of warm cider. After a few sips, Susanna handed it back.

"You haven't slept enough."

She'd slept as long as she could risk. Every second gouged at her heart, the pain a constant ache within.

"Will Father Haden agree, do you think?" she asked, turning to watch the housekeeper.

"Of course he will. That painting you did of him and the Worshipful Company of Plumbers made them all your servants for life, my lady."

"I would think he would do it because Parker is in danger."

"Aye. That, too." Mistress Greene picked up a rag and began wiping down her table. "But do not think you are without influence. You are no longer the stranger you were in these parts. People respect you. And they like you."

Susanna blinked her eyes, then squeezed them shut for a moment. "Thank you."

She had not been here very long, and she was surprised how quickly she had settled in, how much she felt at ease. She thought it was Parker, but of course it was not only him. It was everyone she had dealings with.

"Hoy!"

The shout from across the courtyard had her spinning back to the door, and she saw Harry and Peter Jack running, a large cloth held over their heads.

They each carried a bundle under an arm, and stopped under the eaves of the stable.

"He agreed?" She was breathless with nerves.

"Aye." Peter Jack shouted to be heard over the rain. "He loaned us four, more than we need."

He pushed the stable door open and stepped inside, Harry right behind him.

She looked over her shoulder at Mistress Greene. "Farewell."

She stepped outside and ran to the stable door, leaping the puddles, then stepped into the building's warm, dark air.

Eric stood with the cart, his face set. She knew he had accepted that he could not come with them, but he would not forgive them lightly for it.

"Thank you, Eric." She did not say anything else to him. Nothing would do.

She had felt the same way countless times when her brother had been given a chance or a commission, and she had been overlooked. She knew the slow burn of resentment.

Anything she tried to say to him now, he would take as an insult.

Peter Jack gave her the bundle he carried. She shook it out

and found two cassocks in stiff, scratchy brown wool. "Do we have the belts, as well?"

Harry lifted four rope belts up from his bundle.

She stood, undecided. "Is there a private place between here and St. Sepulchre's where we could don these robes?"

Harry nodded. "There is a small outhouse not far from there; I've used it a time or two."

"Good." She swung up into the cart. "We don't want anyone recognizing us in these too close to home."

"And we don't want them too wet." Harry took the cassocks from her and wrapped all four in a horse blanket.

Eric went to open the stable doors.

The rain had become a shroud over the world, gray and blinding.

"Did you tell Father Haden I plan to wear one?" She couldn't imagine the priest agreeing to it, no matter how much he liked her.

Harry shook his head. "Told him it would be just Peter Jack and me and a couple of my lads." He pulled himself up beside her and took up the reins.

Susanna wondered if Harry had any objection to a woman in priest's clothing. Even the court pageants, with their never-ending themes of disguise and cross-dressing, would not go this far.

Peter Jack climbed in the back, sitting crouched behind them, and drew the heavy, wet cloth he and Harry had used over all of them. Susanna held a corner taut, and Harry flicked the reins.

"Don't—" Eric blocked their way, stopping mid-sentence. He looked too young, his clothes a little too big. Even his eyes, once hard as the streets he'd slept on, looked young. She'd helped soften him, helped to give him expectations of happiness, and now everything hung in the balance.

"We'll be back," she said with conviction.

He looked away, hiding his face. She understood why. He knew better than most that nothing was certain.

# 29

*I hold it to be true that Fortune is the arbiter of one-half of our actions, . . . but that she still leaves us to direct the other half, or perhaps a little less.*

—Machiavelli, The Prince, *chapter 25*

The wool of the cassock felt like a thousand-legged grass-hopper, scratching at Susanna's skin with tiny claws through her fine cotton underclothes.

She'd wrapped the spare robe around her waist underneath it and tied it fast with the rope belt, giving her the appearance of a short, portly monk. She was grateful for the deep cowl that hid her hair and face.

The Church would burn her at the stake if she were caught. Burn her as a witch.

When Harry had suggested this, she had known she couldn't send them into St. Sepulchre's by themselves.

Her family believed in a more inclusive church and was interested in the talk of reforms, but even those broad-minded views weren't enough to stop the feeling of blasphemy as she'd pulled the monk's robes over her head.

Her heart had beat like a bird caught in a trap ever since. As they walked into St. Sepulchre's, every sound, every movement, came to her in stark clarity.

Harry and Peter Jack were beside her, and she could see the tension in their shoulders and faces.

Harry had slipped inside St. Sepulchre's while she and Peter Jack were changing into their robes, and had found the stairs down to the tunnels.

Mass was being said and the chanting echoed through the high chambers, blending and echoing together to form a shimmering net of sound.

Susanna kept to the west side, in deep shadow. The rain had ceased at last and the sun came through the stained glass windows opposite, reaching only far enough to light a quarter of the pews in rainbow colors.

Her feet slowed, then stopped as she took in the scene. She would have to come back and paint this, at exactly this time of day. She wanted to find a way to convey the chanting on canvas, how it became a physical part of the scene. How some of the monks stood bathed in blue, orange, and red, while others were in darkness.

Harry and Peter Jack were a little way in front, and before she moved again to catch up, she saw someone just ahead of them standing in the gloom.

"You." The voice was low, urgent.

Fear skittered over her and she slipped back into the shadows.

The man's hand reached out and grabbed Peter Jack.

"Why aren't you at Mass?" A priest stepped into the half-light, his face impossible to see.

Peter Jack shrugged the hand off. "On an errand, Father." His voice was calm and she felt immensely proud of him.

"What errand?"

Harry stepped closer, crowding in on the priest. He was taller than Peter Jack, broader in the shoulders, and together they made a solid wall. "For the Cardinal."

The priest sucked in a breath. "More of you?" He looked down the outer aisle toward the door to the undercroft. "They did not say there were more of you."

Susanna hoped her shock was not mirrored in Peter Jack and Harry's faces. The Cardinal's men were here?

A sense of urgency rose in her. What could they be doing? She couldn't let go of the notion that they were here to harm Parker. To kill him, perhaps, or take him elsewhere.

The priest indicated the undercroft door, and watched as Harry and Peter Jack walked to it, sure and confident.

She began to move, slipping from pillar to pillar until she was in the darkest part of the aisle, as close to the door as she could get without being seen.

When would the priest go?

Peter Jack turned to look over his shoulder, searching for her. When he saw that the priest had not moved, he gave a nod and stepped through the door after Harry, then closed it behind him.

The priest watched the door, took a hesitant step toward

it . . . then walked forward with more assurance, opened the door, and stepped through.

It swung closed silently.

Susanna stared at the plain, uncarved wood while the monks sang a verse of the liturgy, the sound soaring and swirling up to the high ceiling.

She left the shadows, crossed to the door, and put a hand against it. Then she turned the handle and stepped through.

———————

The stream of sound, the harmony of the chorus, cut off abruptly as she closed the door. She paused on the top step, listening. If the priest had heard the few seconds of increased noise from the church, he might come back to see who had opened the door.

Then again, perhaps he would not.

He'd been standing near the door when Harry and Peter Jack had come upon him, and he had wasted no time following. He could be as false a priest as she was.

Perhaps his talk of Wolsey's men was to scare them off.

The moments ticked by. She'd waited long enough on the landing, and there was no one coming up.

Before she could move down the ill-lit stairs, though, she heard the rustle of fabric brushing against rough stone.

Someone waited just below, on the turn in the staircase.

She stopped breathing, her gaze pinned to the point where anyone climbing the stairs would appear.

Another rustle.

A quick, impatient sound.

And then the sound of footsteps, running lightly down the stairs. Not up.

Wanting to sag against the door in relief, Susanna forced her feet to run down at the same pace, masking the sound of her running with his.

The stairs twisted three times before they ended in a small chamber, stone cold and damp. A lit passage off the room ran roughly south, in the direction of Newgate Prison. Another ran southwest toward the Fleet, but it wasn't lit.

She heard the faint ring of footsteps down the dark tunnel and plunged in after them.

The tunnel swallowed her with one gulp of its shadowed mouth. It consumed her, coated her with obsidian, the color so pure, she wondered what she would do with it if she ever found a pigment this beautifully black.

But there was something amiss. She slowed, frowning, and then stood in the dark, a pulse throbbing at her throat, trying to make sense of it.

She obeyed an impulse to start moving silently backward.

She could track the time she was losing with this compulsion by the drip, drip, drip of water from the ceiling. She timed each step backward with the noise, to make her footsteps even harder to hear.

And then she understood what her senses had been trying to tell her. The footsteps in front of her had stopped, far too long ago. She did not know when.

She'd felt a faint breeze coming down the Newgate tunnel,

chill and unpleasant, with a whiff of night soil about it. But in this dark passageway, no air had stirred at all; it was stale and musty.

Perhaps not a tunnel, then, but a passageway to a cavern, and a neat little trap.

She stumbled, scraping her hand on the rough stone to keep from falling. Harry and Peter Jack could be ahead. Most likely were.

She stopped her backward retreat and listened until her ears buzzed, her eyes creating lights dancing before her in the dark.

At last she heard the sound of someone breathing through their nose. The tiny hairs on her nape and arms rose, and she couldn't suppress the shudder that ran through her.

Someone was ahead, listening, like her. Or waiting for her to stumble into them.

She took a silent step sideways across the passageway, then another, so she was up against the right side rather than the left.

She began to move backward again, feeling the floor for loose rubble before she put her foot down. She found she didn't have the courage to turn her back on whoever was waiting for her.

She heard a soft curse and tensed, standing as still as she could, pressed up hard against the tunnel wall.

The unknown person moved toward her down the tunnel, walking faster than she would have dared in the dark.

She sank down on her haunches, curling herself up as tight as she could. The air moved as he passed her and she thought he was swinging his arms, trying to catch hold of her.

She heard him grunt as he tripped on the uneven floor.

Before he turned the corner she stood and followed him, her hands trembling against the rough stone. She got as close behind him as she dared.

Light bloomed at the tunnel entrance, flickering from the single sconce in the chamber beyond. She could see the man in silhouette, broad at the shoulder, something familiar in the angle of his head.

She needed a place to hide where she could see which way he went, and she began looking for recesses in the wall or a deep shadow to crouch in.

They were almost at the mouth of the tunnel, the flickering light illuminating her various options. She would have to make a choice quickly—

"Ha." He spun, running at her, his arm coming up under her chin as he threw her against the passage wall, pressing down on her throat, cutting off her scream. Her hands scratched at his arm and she kicked out as she hung suspended, choking. She looked him in the face and shock jolted through her.

Jean.

"You." Jean's eyes widened, the light showing his astonishment. He stepped back and her feet hit the ground and she stumbled, bent over, hands to her knees, coughing and whooping as she drew in a breath.

"I am impressed, madame. You have managed to do far more by yourself than I would have thought." He spoke in French, very softly. "But do not let yourself be caught dressed as a monk. You will find even murder is more forgivable than that."

"What are you doing here?" She breathed it out on a whisper of sound, still bent double. Her throat hurt even from that small effort. It was as if something were lodged in it, and she forced back the instinct to retch.

"As you were not convinced of the value of my services, I thought to find your Parker for you anyway. It is always good to negotiate from a position of strength, no?"

"Or you are down here checking on your prisoner?" She had to swallow twice to get the words out and winced as she rubbed a hand over her throat.

"Enough." He grabbed her shoulder, his fingers like a vise. He shook her with only one hand, and she remembered Parker had wounded him. "I will not tell you again that this is not my doing." The pain made her want to cringe away, but she looked him straight in the eye.

"My God, I have never met a more difficult woman." For a second his grip intensified, and if he hadn't needed her, she knew he would have struck her. At last he dropped his hand and took a deep breath.

She moved her shoulder, trying to ease it. The wound on his left shoulder would be a good place to hit him if she needed to later.

"My spies have been following two men who work for the Cardinal. Last night they brought a large bundle between them into this church, and we thought it might be your man."

"Are they here now?" She suddenly remembered what the monk had said above.

Jean shook his head. "I would not be so stupid as to come down with them here."

Susanna shrugged. "The monk who followed my boys down said they were."

Jean froze, then shook his head. "He wanted to put your servants off, perhaps? Make them think it too dangerous?"

Susanna had thought the same, and nodded.

"We are not the only ones who are spying on Wolsey." Jean sheathed a knife in his boot, and Susanna realized she was lucky her throat was not slit. "There is someone else. I was hiding in the Newgate tunnel when your two boys came down. I nearly confronted them, but then the other spy came after them. Someone I don't know."

"Where did they go?"

"Down this passage." Jean jerked his head the way they had just come. "To a dead end. They were sizing each other up when I reached them. I realized there was nothing there and began back. But then I heard you in the passage with me, and we had our game of cat and mouse."

"There is another passage." Susanna did not know when she decided he was telling the truth, but if he was the one who had taken Parker, he knew about the secret tunnel anyway. "A tunnel that comes out inside Fleet Prison."

Jean stepped away from her, his head to the side. Considering.

"There was something . . ." He walked to the tunnel entrance, close to the wall, and looked out into the chamber. When he was sure it was empty, he stepped into the room.

Susanna followed and waited for him as he turned slowly, considering every angle.

"There." He spoke to himself, so softly. Susanna took a step closer to him. She followed his gaze and saw there was a small door in the side of the stairs. It looked like a small storage cupboard.

Jean tried the handle, inching it down. It gave, but did not open.

Locked.

He moved his left arm and cursed, his face white. He'd forgotten he was wounded, just as Parker kept forgetting. He lifted the bag slung across his chest off him and held it out for her.

She opened the bag and he searched through it, one-handed, and drew out a dull metal instrument. He inserted it into the lock and began to work it.

She could see sweat on his upper lip and brow, though the air seemed colder. The sconce lighting flickered and thinned, and she feared it would go out and sink them into darkness.

Jean shivered, and she wondered if he was getting a fever with his injury.

There was a sound from the dark tunnel, the clatter of feet and the bouncing echo of angry voices.

Jean's hand shook, and for the first time since she'd met him, he seemed nervous, rattled.

"It's Harry and Peter Jack, most likely. They can help us."

"And whoever is with them? Do you want them to know of this passageway, too?" His words were harsh and low, his eyes flicking to the tunnel as his hand moved and twisted the metal in the lock.

Susanna heard a click, but when Jean tried the handle again, it did not budge.

He lost his patience and rattled the pick, then took a deep breath and moved it again, carefully. There was another click, and then another.

The voices were getting louder, harsher. At least Harry and Peter Jack were safe, and arguing, by the sound of things.

They were coming around the corner.

"Get that light," Jean hissed, and Susanna ran and lifted it off the wall just as he opened the door.

She sprinted across the chamber, monk's robes flying around her, and followed Jean inside. As she stepped through he closed the door, and the boys and their adversary burst into the chamber.

"Where's the light?"

It was Harry, and she could hear the edge of exhaustion in his voice.

"Someone has taken it. Most likely down the Newgate tunnel." It was the man from earlier.

Their footsteps thumped on the stairs as they went up, and then there was silence.

"And now?" Susanna lifted the torch and saw a tunnel stretching out before them.

"Now we look for your Parker." Jean lifted a hand to his shoulder. "I have much to discuss with him."

# 30

*I compare her to one of those raging rivers, which when
in flood overflows the plains, sweeping away trees and
buildings, bearing away the soil from place to place; everything flies before it, all yield to its violence, without
being able in any way to withstand it.*

—Machiavelli, The Prince, chapter 25

Susanna did not trust Jean and she didn't like him, but
she was glad he was with her. She wouldn't have found
the tunnel, and she wouldn't have liked walking down it on
her own.

It should put her in his debt—but he had tried to kill her
once, and had murdered Jens. She felt no obligation to him.

He had been too quick for her earlier in the tunnel, and
she hadn't had a chance to get to her knife, but now she was
glad she had not shown it.

It would be a good surprise for later, if she needed it.

She rubbed her throat again, fighting the urge to cough.
Neither of them made a sound, and Susanna thought she
heard a noise ahead. A rhythmic banging.

Jean tapped her shoulder, and she looked at him to find his finger on his lips.

He had heard it, too.

Their pace slowed, and Jean unclipped his crossbow from his belt and held it awkwardly in his right hand.

Susanna shook her right arm, and felt her knife hilt nudge her palm.

The banging was louder now, and more erratic. Not the steady rhythm of a hammer, more like the thump of a body against a solid object. Like someone throwing themselves against a door.

"Parker." Her cry echoed down the tunnel, bounding and rebounding, and Jean looked back at her with horror.

"Are you mad?" He lifted the crossbow in a sharp, furious movement, pointing it straight down the tunnel, and moved faster.

The noise stopped, too abruptly to be coincidence.

Her cry had been heard by someone.

"Parker!" It hurt so much to shout, it was as if someone had run a knife tip down the inside of her throat. It brought tears to her eyes.

She heard a shout in return, muffled but audible. Then a sound like a fist pounding.

Susanna ran, the torch flickering wildly as she sprinted down the passageway. She pushed Jean aside and could sense him at her shoulder, his silence cold and angry.

The tunnel opened up suddenly without warning, and Susanna stumbled to a halt. The short, wide section contained three doors on each side before it narrowed again and disappeared toward the Fleet.

The walls were of natural stone; she guessed the tunnel diggers had come across a natural chamber and decided to make use of it.

"Parker?"

There was a bang against the middle right door, and she ran to it and banged back. "Where is your lock pick?" Her voice broke as she called to Jean. She grabbed hold of the door handle and tugged. It rattled a little. Parker had weakened it.

Jean said nothing, and she turned, frowning. He was standing with his crossbow held loosely away from his body, but in a way that told her he could lift it and fire at any moment.

"I think now is a good time to negotiate, hmm?"

---

When Parker first heard her call, he thought he was hearing things. The pain in his body from every smash of his shoulder against the door made him light-headed, and he was sure, even though he stopped to listen, that it could not be her.

When her shout came again, his legs collapsed under him. He raised a fist and banged it on the door, too exhausted to call out.

The answering bang gave him the strength he needed to pull himself up.

He heard Susanna demanding something of someone, and then silence.

There was a sound in the lock, the snick and grind of metal on metal, and Parker realized someone was picking it.

The movements were quick and efficient, and as the door swung outward he pushed himself through, so unsteady on his feet, he knocked whoever had opened it to one side.

He came to an abrupt halt. Susanna stood in the middle of the room dressed as a monk, with a torch in one hand. He blinked to clear his vision, trying to make sense of what he saw.

The man he'd pushed aside moved directly in front of him, and for a long moment, Parker and the French assassin stared at each other.

Parker could see amusement and arrogance in the Frenchman's eyes; there was only shock in his.

The Frenchman's lips curled up, and his eyes moved to Susanna. He lunged for her, but she thrust the torch in his face and he leaped back, cursing.

Parker moved in an arc, each step an effort to stay upright. He kept the Frenchman in view and reached Susanna's side. She said nothing, her gaze going to him, eyes glittering in the torchlight. She switched the torch to her left hand and flicked her right, then held out the knife that landed in her palm.

His eyes still on the Frenchman, he kissed the top of her head as he took it. Not that he could best a crossbow with a knife.

Both of his arms felt encased in scorching lead. It would be almost impossible to lift one and throw the knife accurately against the aim of a bolt pointed at his heart.

"You do not look well." The Frenchman moved, shifting his bow, and Parker remembered he'd injured him. It was only mild consolation as the bolt tip leveled with his chest again.

"I am well enough." It was a lie, and they all knew it.

There was the clang of a gate from deeper down the tunnel, and all three froze, listening.

"Mistress Horenbout has made me certain promises, and perhaps, now that I have you trapped between whoever is coming from the other side and my crossbow, I can ask that you both come with me now to fulfil them."

Parker glanced at Susanna and saw her lips thin and her eyes narrow. She blew out a breath.

The Frenchman raised an eyebrow, looked over Susanna's shoulder to the passage beyond, and then back to both of them, the question clear.

They could all hear the heavy tread of footsteps, and someone began to whistle tunelessly.

Susanna lifted her cowl to cover her face.

The steps came closer.

"What have you promised him?" Parker asked her.

She gave him a sidelong look. "He wants me to retrieve the Mirror of Naples for him, from where Jens left it." Her voice was husky, faint.

He absorbed her words with difficulty, unable to take his eyes off her, but her attention was already back on the Frenchman.

The assassin took a step toward the tunnel. "They are almost upon us. Let's go." His agitation was clear. He would not like to be caught down here by the wardens of the Fleet any more than they would.

Parker didn't know how fast he could run, even as he readied himself for whatever Susanna had in mind.

He sensed the Frenchman tensing as the footsteps sounded closer.

"We will not go with you." Susanna's voice was hoarse, as if her throat had been injured. He could no longer see her face, shadowed by the deep cowl, but her grip on the torch tightened.

"You are merely delaying the inevitable." The Frenchman couldn't control the anger in his tone. Parker sensed there was something between him and Susanna, some conflict he knew nothing about.

She shook her head and lifted her hands, the movement unhurried and dismissive, and he cursed.

"I'll be waiting for you farther down the tunnel when you come to your senses and run. If you try to escape past me without honoring your promise, I *will* shoot."

He backed away, disappearing into the darkness, the tip of the bolt the last thing to be swallowed by the shadows.

Parker turned to Susanna and stood swaying, beyond words, as she loosened the rope belt of her monk's robe and lifted it up.

Beneath it, there was something tied around her waist—another monk's robe. She pulled it loose and handed it to him, along with the belt that had held it around her midriff.

Parker couldn't put them on. He could not lift his arms.

Susanna tied the rope belt around her again, and then looked up sharply when she realized he was not dressing.

"I can't lift—"

The footsteps sounded as if they were just around the corner.

She lunged forward and grabbed the robe and rope, snatching the knife from his hand. In its place she handed him the torch.

As the world tilted and dipped around him, Parker felt as if everything happened at half speed.

Susanna spun into the dark corner where the tunnel opened into the natural chamber, and as she pressed herself against the wall, a man stepped through and tripped over his feet at the sight of Parker standing with a flickering torch in his hand.

"What . . ." The word was whispered, then he took a deep breath as if to shout.

Susanna leaped out, robe in hand, and brought the brown wool over the man's eyes. He crumpled as if she'd knocked the back of his legs to unbalance him, and as he hit the ground with his knees, hands out to save himself, she looped the rope around his head and tied it tight, turning the robe into a hood.

She brought the knife up to his throat and let him feel the tip through the wool.

He flinched.

"Stay very still." Her words were whispered, the sound eerie in the echoing chamber. She kept the knife pressed against his skin and tugged at the belt around his waist. "Undo your belt."

The man's fingers fumbled with the task, and a moment later the belt—heavy with jangling keys—was in Susanna's hands.

"Now move. On your hands and knees, move forward." The man moved awkwardly, and with the knife still pricking him, Susanna walked beside him, nudging him in the direction of Parker's cell.

When he crossed the threshold she slammed the door shut and flipped through the keys, working fast as the man hammered at the door.

She found the right key and turned it in the lock with an audible click, and for a heartbeat there was silence.

Then the man began to pound the door again and shout, the sound muffled.

"Come." She walked to Parker and took his arm, as gentle now as she had been ferocious a moment before.

His skin was hot and tight, yet he was cold to his core and shivering. He tried to focus, to concentrate, but his mind would not settle.

Susanna gave his arm a tug. "I am tired of this, Parker. I want it to end. And if I have to behave a little like you to do it, then I will." She took the torch from him and towed him behind her, her stride steady and sure.

They came to an iron gate blocking the tunnel from floor to ceiling. Susanna tried two keys before she opened it. She did not close and lock it behind her.

There was a stench here, a smell that seemed ingrained in the very stone around them. Parker sensed the darkness, the despair, from a long way off. He was apart from his body, content to allow Susanna to lead him where she would.

Their steps elicited cries and calls all around them, and Parker squinted to focus. There were cells on either side of them now, and Susanna stopped at each one, unlocking the doors.

"Is this Bartholomew Fair?" Her whisper echoed through the passage.

He heard a few cries of assent, and she continued down the tunnel, unlocking as she went.

A small group of men emerged from their holes, twitchy and nervous. They began to follow her as though she were a fairy-tale piper.

"Go the other way." She pointed in the direction they had just come. "There is a man down there with a crossbow, but if you call out who you are, he will not harm you. It is only us he wants to kill."

"Where does the tunnel lead?" A man stepped out of a cell, filthy and wild, his hair standing in stiff tufts, his face a blackened mess with white, staring eyes.

With a vague sense of recognition, Parker tilted his head to look more closely; he thought the man might be some minor figure from court.

"St. Sepulchre's." Susanna turned away and moved on, tugging Parker along.

"Is that you, Parker?" The man moved away from his cell cautiously, as if expecting the world to dissolve around him.

Speaking was too much effort, so Parker merely raised a hand. It bothered him he did not know the man's name, but if this was the Fleet, then most of these prisoners would be men who had annoyed the nobles in power, or Wolsey.

He stumbled as they reached a staircase, blocked by another gate, and Susanna did lock this one behind them before helping him up each step as if he were a small child.

"Eh?" A man blocked the way at the top of the stairs. Susanna's face was in deep shadow, and she had somehow tucked his cloak back so his chain of office was in full view.

"Out of the way." She spoke in a clipped whisper, and the man obliged, too surprised to do anything else.

Parker tried to draw himself up, to tower over the shorter man, but he had no sense of whether he had managed to or not. He had a curious floating sensation, and kept having to juggle his feet to keep from staggering sideways.

There was another strong door ahead.

"Where'd you come from?" The warden's voice was neutral. He wasn't sure whether to be respectful or not.

Parker saw he was torn between going down the stairs to see what they had been up to below, and following them. They were a priest and a king's officer, and he was obliged to obey them, but they shouldn't be here.

Susanna took advantage of his uncertainty, searching through the keys and trying one with a shaking hand. "One of your men is injured below." She spoke matter-of-factly, her voice rough and low, and Parker turned his head to the man and saw him frown.

"I think a prisoner harmed him."

The warden kept his gaze on them but took the first few steps down the stairs, and Parker heard the click as a key turned the lock. Susanna fumbled a little as she drew the key out and swung open the door, pulled him through, and slammed it behind them, locking it in one deft movement.

They were in a large open yard, surrounded by the crenellated walls of the Fleet Prison. The massive doors to the outside were straight ahead, and Susanna walked directly toward them. Parker had the sense of being very small in a massive space, of having some terrible power hovering just over them, ready to crush them on a whim.

"Stop." A man waddled out of a side building, his belly hanging over his belt, his face unwashed and unshaven. His eyes seemed unusually small in his face, but they gleamed bright.

"We will let ourselves out. No need for you to be distracted from your . . . work." Susanna's voice was thready, almost gone, making her sound strangely sinister.

The man looked between them, a frown creasing deep lines in his forehead.

"The Star Chamber is expecting our report as soon as possible, so we will bid you good day."

The warden stepped back a little, clearly perturbed by the way she spoke in a whisper.

She lifted the keys, selected the largest one, and walked toward a smaller door cut into the large gate.

"I didn't know anything about a report." The man moved alongside them, shuffling his feet to keep up.

"It would not be an accurate report on the state of the Fleet if you *had* known of it, would it?" Susanna did not slow down.

"But . . ."

Parker kept his gaze on the man's face, watching for some warning if he decided to attack, but all he saw was horror.

"Good day." Susanna spoke the words without turning around. She turned the key in the door, and Parker realized vaguely it had opened.

She pulled him out, closed the door and locked it behind them, and then grabbed his arm again. Her hands were shaking so badly, he could feel each shiver. "Let's get as far away from here as we can."

# 31

*Pretexts for taking away property are never wanting; for he who has once begun to live by robbery will always find pretexts for seizing what belongs to others; but reasons for taking life, on the contrary, are more difficult to find and sooner lapse.*

—Machiavelli, The Prince, *chapter 17*

Dusk had fallen, and the bells of St. Michael's had rung before Maggie was finished at Parker's house.

"I thought I told you to lock him up." The healer's words held no heat; she knew full well the impossibility of such an order.

Susanna closed her eyes and rested her head against her fists on Mistress Greene's kitchen table, too exhausted to do anything more than sit.

"You need me to tend to you?" Maggie's voice sharpened, and Susanna looked up as she shook her head.

"Just tired. And my throat." Her voice was still husky, but the two cups of honey and lemon tea Mistress Greene had given her had restored it a little.

"Put this salve on it to help the bruising." Maggie placed a small wooden box on the table beside her.

Susanna nodded her thanks, and saw a look pass between the healer and Mistress Greene as she lifted the lid and dipped a finger into the salve.

The air filled with a strong herbal perfume as the door closed behind Maggie.

The housekeeper said, "She doesn't think it wise for you to go after Harry and Peter Jack. You need rest. Let the boys do it. Harry is theirs. They want to, anyway."

Susanna rubbed the mixture onto her throat with delicate upward strokes. The salve had a cooling property, and she dipped her finger into the box again. "Harry's boys can help me, but I can't go to sleep without knowing where they are."

"No doubt they're running themselves ragged trying to find you."

Susanna hoped that was so. She closed the lid and forced herself to her feet. "Where are the lads, then?"

"With Eric out in the stables. You'll have a hard time keeping Eric back. He's set on going along."

Susanna nodded; she would expect nothing less. She drew on her cloak. "I don't know when I'll be back, but if Parker should ask . . ."

Mistress Greene set her mouth. "I'll not lie."

Susanna walked to her and put a hand on each shoulder. "I don't expect you to." She felt an overwhelming need to rest her head on Mistress Greene's softly rounded breasts, to be led to bed and tucked in.

She snapped up, blinking her eyes and breathing deep to get her body awake again. "Tell Parker where I've gone. I'll send a lad back every hour with news, if I can."

"That would be appreciated." Mistress Greene gave a sniff. As she turned, Susanna saw a tear glimmering in her eye.

She opened the back door, and for once welcomed the bracing cold wind as it lifted her cloak. It ripped the warmth and the lethargy from her, and she stepped into the backyard with more energy than she'd had since Parker had fallen asleep.

Dusk had darkened to early evening, and she had a bitter enemy to face.

———————

"Mistress Horenbout, I see you are not your usual serene self."

Susanna huddled deep in her cloak, having refused to give it up when she'd entered Norfolk's house. She hoped she was up to dealing with the most cunning and powerful man in England, after Wolsey and the King.

"It has been a trying day for me, Your Grace. I have a feeling some of my troubles may be known to you. The man in the monk's robes at St. Sepulchre's must have told you some of it."

She watched him carefully and saw him flinch a little at the mention of St. Sepulchre's. His man had not seen her. Norfolk must be wondering how she knew.

He pretended ignorance. "St. Sepulchre's?"

Ready for this, she held out a quick sketch. It was of Norfolk's spy in his monk's robes.

Norfolk's eyes narrowed. "Whatever else I think of you, mistress, you are uncanny fine in your picture making."

"Where did he go, and what did he do with my pages?"

"I am surprised you would come here alone, without Parker. If he thought I had something to do with the disappearance of his pages, he would be here holding a knife to my throat, or some other crude gesture."

"That is true." Susanna did not allow her gaze to falter. "While Parker is busy elsewhere, I have taken action on my own. But if you would like Parker and his methods here instead of me and mine, that can be arranged."

Norfolk raised a brow. "The way I've heard it, Parker is nowhere to be found."

Susanna stared him down. "You have heard it wrong."

He seemed to weigh up whether to believe her or not. Eventually, he shrugged. "I have no use for your pages. They should be at St. Sepulchre's."

A hot, heavy claw closed around her gut and squeezed. "I have already been to St. Sepulchre's." *And they were not there.*

"Then I cannot help you." He did not look ready for her to leave, though. He drummed his fingers against the dark wood of his desk, and watched her from under hooded lids. "The French seem very interested in you, I've noticed."

Susanna remembered him watching her in the King's chamber and stilled, like a bird ready to burst into flight as soon as the hound leaped. "The French are not interested in me at all."

"That is untrue. Why, the Comte seemed most taken by you the other night."

"You did not watch closely enough, then. He was anything but taken by me."

"Mmmm." Norfolk took up a quill and tilted it back and forth between his fingers. "I noticed you enraged him as much as you have enraged me in the past, but not many others did. They saw only your arm in his grasp. The special attention he gave you. And noted, as I did, that he left soon after you."

"By then," Susanna said sweetly, "I was in audience with the Queen. I think she will be quite a difficult witness to naysay."

Norfolk snapped the quill. "Indeed. But whether you met with him afterward or not, the scene was noted by enough for my purpose."

"And what is your purpose?" She could hear the double thump of her heart in her chest.

"I want Wolsey gone. Ruined. I know what he's been up to. If you interfere with my plans to expose him, I will serve you up on a platter to the Tower for treason with as much fabricated evidence as I can get away with."

They stared at each other.

"And I will not have to fabricate much, after that scene with the Comte."

Susanna had no answer to that. Nothing she said would change anything, so she turned and walked out of his study, out into the hallway and out the front door.

Headed for the only other place the boys could be: with the French.

# 32

*And in examining their actions and lives one cannot see
that they owed anything to fortune beyond opportunity,
which brought them the material to mould into the form
which seemed best to them. Without that opportunity
their powers of mind would have been extinguished, and
without those powers the opportunity would have come
in vain.*

—Machiavelli, The Prince, *chapter 6*

"You have quite a nerve, madame." The Comte stood high
on the staircase, looking down on Susanna. "To come
knocking on my door, you must be bold as a street whore."

"You have forced me to boldness." Susanna kept her head
raised. "You have my pages. By coming to you I'm merely
saving you time."

She heard a sound to her right, turned her head, and saw Jean
leaning against the door of a large room off the main entrance.

"Saving us time?" Jean's eyes were hot and his fists were
clenched.

Susanna felt her throat close and had to clear it to speak.
"I am sure your spies are still wasting time trying to find out if
Parker and I are in the tunnel, or in the Fleet."

She stood with her feet planted apart and cocked her head, as aggressive as any of the street whores she'd seen. She wished for a tenth of their bravado and negotiating skills now. She certainly had their desperation. "You should be happy I'm here. Your holding Harry and Peter Jack is only useful if I'm free and in a position to give you what you want."

Jean spat. From the corner of her eye, Susanna saw the Comte wince. "Your word is nothing to me. You made a promise in the tunnel and then you refused to honor it."

She did not look away. "I do not deny it. At the moment I made the promise, I had no choice. Then I did have a choice."

"The Fleet was a choice?" The Comte's voice was disbelieving.

"You think I'm mad?" Her voice cracked on the last few words and she swallowed hard, wishing for something to drink to soothe it. "Yet *your* request is mad. You ask me to give up my reputation, the reputation of my betrothed, and possibly my life. The Fleet was most certainly a choice."

"You took the risk that you could walk out of one of the most guarded prisons in England, instead of doing what I asked, but will give in to me for the lives of two servants?" The Comte shook his head, as if not sure what to make of her.

"So, you will come with us now? And try to find the Mirror?" Jean straightened. "When we have it, we will release your boys."

"No." It came out a croak. Susanna swallowed again. "When we get wherever you need me to be, I will go inside only if I see my pages released right there, free to run off."

"Why would we agree to that?"

"Because there is a chance I may be caught." Susanna crossed her arms under her breasts. "They should be free no matter what happens to me."

"*Bien.* I agree." The Comte waved a hand. "Let's go."

Susanna half-turned to the door, then hesitated.

"What is it?" Jean was already level with her.

"The Duke of Norfolk. He is watching me. If he thinks I'm going to interfere with his plans, he will try to have me sent to the Tower."

"What are his plans?" The Comte had reached the bottom of the stairs, and there was no mistaking the interest in his eyes.

"To bring down Wolsey."

"That is unfortunate." Jean shrugged, but Susanna thought there was a trace of glee in the movement.

"More than unfortunate." The Comte spoke sharply. "If Norfolk watches her too closely, he watches us."

"His spies *are* watching me. They may have followed me here."

"Then Jean will have to make sure they do not report back to their master. We also do not want any interference." The Comte stood by the door, but did not open it. "Perhaps we can take the side door, madame? Jean, make sure the Duke's men do not follow. By any means."

Jean flicked an angry look at her. "You are sure there is danger from Norfolk?"

"I know there is." She felt a tug of guilt at the fate of the men the Duke would have sent after her, even though she'd had more than one unpleasant encounter with his servants.

Jean turned toward the back of the house. He seemed to slice the darkness and slip through the hole, disappearing in one swallow of the shadows.

The Comte watched him go, and kept watching the darkened passageway until the last of his footsteps faded. Only then did he relax.

"You put him on edge." He gestured in bewilderment. "There is something about you that enrages him. He is not his collected self when you are present."

"You think it is safer for me that he does not accompany us?"

The Comte started down the passage, stopping in front of the side door. "If you have made an enemy of Jean, nowhere is safe for you anymore."

———————

The softness and the scent that cocooned Parker were of home, and as he fought his way to wakefulness, he reveled in the simple comfort.

He had never taken what he had gained for himself lightly. Wealth, fine clothes and lodgings, servants. But he felt an even deeper appreciation for them since his stay in the foul chambers beneath Fleet Prison.

As he surfaced, he was content to keep his eyes closed and listen to the sounds of the house around him. The soft creak of the roof in the wind. The buzz of vibration as the gale forced itself between the wooden shutters.

He could hear Mistress Greene in the kitchen, banging pans, and the slam of the back door as it was caught by the wind.

There was another clatter, and he frowned. He had never known Mistress Greene to be so noisy, not even when he was in perfect health. And if any of them were laid up for any reason, she was always obsessively quiet.

The back door slammed again and Parker sat up in a swift movement, his heart suddenly thundering.

Susanna.

That was what woke him.

He could not hear her. Could not sense her.

She was not in the house.

There were many men at court whose wives would not sit beside them in illness. Some even socialized while their husbands lay sick and dying.

But she was not one of them.

If she was in the house, she would be here in this room.

And she wasn't.

It sounded as if Mistress Greene threw a copper pot at the wall. He heard the crash and then the ting as it bounced on the stone floor of the kitchen, the rumble as it spun and slowly came to a stop.

Parker swung his feet to the floor, and closed his eyes against the wave of dizziness that pushed him back onto the bed.

He aimed himself at the door, staggered through it, and grabbed hold of the banister at the top of the landing.

He looked down the stairs straight into the desperate, wild eyes of Mistress Greene, holding a copper bowl over her head, ready to throw.

She lowered the bowl. "Thank the heavens."

"Where is Susanna?" He couldn't believe his voice sounded so calm.

"She's gone and thrown herself to the wolves, sir. To get back those boys."

# 33

*For my part I consider that it is better to be adventurous than cautious, because fortune is a woman, and if you wish to keep her under it is necessary to beat and ill-use her; and it is seen that she allows herself to be mastered by the adventurous rather than by those who go to work more coldly.*

—Machiavelli, The Prince, *chapter 25*

Susanna saw Westminster up around the bend, and her stomach pitched along with the small barge she was in.

She suddenly knew where the jewel was. Knew down to the very room.

She closed her eyes and recalled the numbers and notes on the inventory. It was possible she even knew exactly where to look, down to the precise box.

The wind hit them full force, slicing at her face and ears. It carried a hint of ice and snow, and a shiver ran through her.

She glanced at the Comte, who had wrapped his cloak tighter about him, his eyes on the spires of Westminster Abbey. Did he know the precise location, too?

She gripped her cloak in her fists. How should she play this out?

She'd hoped to be able to say truthfully that she could not find the Mirror.

She looked behind her and saw Harry's eyes, fury and frustration distilled in their gray.

The man the Comte had brought with him to manage the boys raised his brows at her, but she ignored him.

Harry and Peter Jack lay bound and gagged at the bottom of the boat. Peter Jack moved a little, turning toward her, and his watcher placed a heavy boot on his throat. Clicked his tongue.

Susanna faced forward again before she stirred up trouble.

The boys had not gone quietly. Their knuckles were scraped and raw, their faces bruised. But they seemed otherwise all right, and she held the bargaining chip when it came to their release.

She knew the Comte could send his men after them once they were set free, but at least they would have a chance.

"Where in Westminster do you think the Mirror is hidden?" She asked the question as if she were passing the time of day.

The Comte turned eyes watery with the cold wind to her. "I will tell you when we are there."

She shrugged and forced her hands to relax on her lap.

When the barge scraped against the dock, she got up with relief and took the hand offered by the Comte's boatman.

The boys' minder untied them and they sat up slowly, rubbing their wrists and ankles to get the blood circulating. They filed off the boat, shaky and quiet.

"You can both be home with Parker in half an hour, if you're quick." She spoke softly and without emphasis, trying not to draw attention to what she was saying.

But Harry and Peter Jack both understood. The light returned to Harry's eyes at the thought of Parker being safe and home, and Peter Jack stared at her.

"You foun—"

"I would start running if I were you." The Comte waved them off as if they were flies and turned Susanna away from them, making her face Westminster.

She stiffened and turned back. "No. I will see that they are safely away." The boys hobbled toward the road, looking over their shoulders, as if to keep her in sight until the very last.

"They are safe enough." The Comte took her by the arm and she could feel his anger and frustration as he spun her back.

"What would you have me do?" She relaxed her body, and his grip fell away.

"I would have you find Jens's quarters."

"Jens stayed here?" Susanna could not keep the surprise from her voice.

"He did." There was rich satisfaction in the Comte's tone. "And I think he hid the Mirror somewhere in his room, or near it."

"If he was staying here, why could he not get the Mirror whenever he wanted?"

"Because," the Comte said, "in all his wisdom, the Cardinal had him thrown out and refused to let him back in."

"And what makes you think I will have access to his chambers?" Susanna braced against another gust of wind.

The Comte laughed. "Your betrothed is the Keeper of this palace. There is nowhere here you cannot go."

It was true. She had been here enough in Parker's company that the guards would recognize her and let her through.

"Am I going alone?"

A smile played on the Comte's face. "You think, after all the times you have reneged on us, I would trust you to look properly?"

Susanna shrugged and said nothing.

"You will have a page with you. He will meet you when you gain entrance."

"If you have someone inside the palace already, why do you need me?"

"He is only kitchen staff, and cannot go anywhere else."

"How long have you had a spy in Westminster?" Susanna began moving forward to get out of the wind.

The Comte's voice dripped bitterness. "Since the Mirror of Naples was stolen from France."

---

"Hi! Sir!"

Parker stopped the cart as he turned out of the yard into Crooked Lane, and waited for the small boy to catch up.

"Thought you were in your sickbed?" The lad swung up onto the bench, his cheeks stung red by the wind.

Parker shook his head. "What news?"

"I'm to watch the house, and if Harry and Peter Jack come back, I'm to pass the message on."

"Where is Eric?"

"Don't know." The lad pointed down to Fish Hill. "Will is waiting down there; he's part of the chain."

"The chain?"

"There's a string of us, sir. Eric's at the pointy end." The boy jumped down. "Need to get back to my post."

He ran back up to the house, and Parker sped up, trying to spot Will at the junction of Crooked Lane and Fish Hill.

He saw him immediately, standing beside a tavern, giving a good impression of a page waiting while his master went in for a drink.

Parker caught his eye and he ran across, hunching against the wind.

"Thought you was hurt?"

Parker grimaced. "Where's Mistress Horenbout, Will?"

He shrugged. "Eric's watching her back."

"Which way?"

Will pointed up Fish Hill. "The Comte's house. That's where they went first. Not sure where they are now."

Parker nodded his thanks and forced the horse into a trot up the hill. It was already dark and the wind had culled the usual market crowds, so he made good progress.

He pushed all thoughts of pain away, despite the sharp

stabs of agony in both shoulders, and turned left toward the Comte's mansion.

Susanna had gone back on her bargain with Jean once before, and Parker knew she would try anything in her power to do it again.

Jean must know it, too.

She would be under guard. The thought of Jean having any power over her made him flick the reins again, even though the horse could go no faster.

He was almost there.

A dart of movement ahead caught his attention. It was panicked, the movement of a mouse with a cat after it, and he slowed the cart.

He had not seen who it was, and they had gone to ground in the deep shadows.

"Eric?" The gate to the Comte's residence was directly to his right. The panic in the moment he'd seen was not a good sign.

Down the long drive to the Comte's mansion, someone screamed, and Parker jumped from the cart, leaving it in the middle of the street.

He palmed his knife and slipped between the trees. It was the way he'd come the day Wolsey's men had taken him while he watched the Comte's front door. He had no intention of being taken by surprise again.

Whoever had run between the Comte's drive and the next stand of houses was behind him, and although he'd gotten the impression of a boy, he kept a careful watch.

The scream had gone on, a long, continuous wail that grabbed the back of his neck in a chilly grasp. It cut off sharply, and Parker moved forward as fast as he could in the silence.

It was the silence after life has been taken. When the hunter has shot his arrow and the deer has finished struggling and now lies still. The hair on his arms rose, as if a shade brushed over him as it left the world behind, and he shivered.

He crouched low as he came to the edge of the trees, the house in view. Some of the lower-floor windows were lit, casting a glow around the mansion that wavered and flickered with the candles within, a swirling, diaphanous skirt of light.

He readied himself to take a chance and run to a window to look in, to see if Susanna could be there, but before he took the first step, a shadow rose up from beneath a window.

Jean.

A twig snapped behind him, and someone fell heavily on the ground.

Jean turned, unerring as a bloodhound, and Parker saw him lift his crossbow up.

Crouched low, Parker tried to beat Jean to the source of the noise, but froze low and deep in the undergrowth as Jean passed by.

He heard a scuffle and straightened up, edging forward until he stood right behind Jean.

In the dim light filtering between the trees, he saw that the assassin had a young boy cowering on the ground, and that his crossbow was raised and aimed.

"Who do you work for?"

The boy was silent. Parker recognized him as James, one of the lads who worked for Harry.

Jean sighed, sighted the bow, and Parker realized he was about to kill. Moving faster than he thought possible, he pressed his knife to Jean's throat, and satisfaction sang in his blood.

He fought the urge to cut deep.

"Killing children, now, Jean?"

"Killing Norfolk's spies." Jean did not betray any surprise at the sound of Parker's voice. "Though I thought I'd got them all after that last one."

"This one isn't Norfolk's, he's mine."

"Ah." There was silence a moment. "I wondered where you were, earlier, when your lady came round."

"Why are you killing Norfolk's men?"

Jean turned his head a little, and Parker saw his lip curl in distaste. "They were following your lady. The Comte does not want Norfolk privy to our plans."

Fear thrust a cold hand down Parker's back. He had spent too much time on the French, and had ignored Norfolk at his cost. If the Duke had evidence that Susanna was conspiring with the French, whether willingly or not, he would use it. If not in this affair, then some other time.

"Where is my betrothed?"

James had risen, standing tense as a wild animal, ready to run. He opened his mouth to talk, but Parker gave the smallest shake of his head.

He let the blade dig deeper into Jean's neck. "Is she inside?"

Jean said nothing.

"Perhaps we should go and look?" Parker grabbed the back of Jean's doublet and shoved him forward, but instead of resisting, Jean threw himself at the ground, twisting midair as he did, crossbow up.

Parker dropped down and felt a rush of air as a bolt brushed past him.

Jean cried out in pain as he hit the ground on his damaged shoulder. He rolled to his feet and staggered into the undergrowth.

"Do we go after him?" James stood where he was and watched Parker with wide eyes.

Parker shook his head. "Where is Susanna?"

"Took her out the side way, they did. Then down to the river, to a barge. I came back here to see why that Frenchman didn't go with them." James's teeth started to chatter. "Tripped over the first body in the half-light. Shot through the back." He shuddered, as if to try to shake loose the memory.

"Did they go up- or downriver?"

"Upriver. Eric is following, running the bank to keep them in sight."

"Are there other lads along the way? Anyone who can tell me where they put in?"

James shook his head. "'Twas just me and Eric left. The rest are out looking for Harry and Peter Jack. I best tell 'em they were in the barge with your lady. Carried out behind 'er like two lumps, they were. All tied up 'n' knocked about."

Parker cast a last glance at the house. It was dangerous leaving Jean free, but every moment might count for Susanna. He couldn't risk the delay.

"What will you do, sir?"

Parker thought of the boatmen from the time he'd shot the bridge. "I think it's time to call on some old friends."

# 34

*It is not unknown to me how many men have had, and
still have, the opinion that the affairs of the world are in
such wise governed by fortune and by God that men
with their wisdom cannot direct them and that no one
can even help them; and because of this they would have
us believe that it is not necessary to labour much in affairs, but to let chance govern them.*

—Machiavelli, The Prince, *chapter 25*

Every step she took was a betrayal of trust.

She nodded to the guards, who bowed and let her
through, the wife-to-be of their master.

That Parker would approve what she did didn't help ease
the nausea that roiled in her stomach.

She let the page guide her through the passageways, although he slipped behind her whenever they came upon
someone about their business. His head no doubt subservi-
ently bowed.

She had not spoken a word to him. He was young, but too
old to be a page, and he bowed and cringed to make himself
smaller.

She could see a quickness and an intelligence in his face,

and thought he wouldn't have gone unnoticed in the palace for long.

He and the Comte thought they would find the Mirror tonight and be done and gone. They were in for a disappointment.

"We need to go through here." For the first time, he tugged his cowl over his head before they turned the corner.

Susanna steeled herself to smile and nod at more guards, but although there was a place for them at the entrance to the wing, they were not there.

"There have always been guards here." The French spy's words set a spider of fear crawling across Susanna's neck.

She surged ahead to shake it off, and the Frenchman followed her.

The corridor held accommodations for the more senior servants of the nobles at court. Had she needed a room at court, she would most likely have found herself in one of these.

They were small but private, and one drew the eye because its door was hanging off a single hinge. With heart pounding, Susanna approached the entrance, and looked in on mayhem.

Someone had ripped every item in the room to shreds, and what could not be ripped had been smashed.

"Mon Dieu." The Frenchman stepped inside and looked around with bleak eyes. "If there was anything here, someone else has it now."

Susanna crouched down and picked up a broken

wooden box. There was nothing inside it, and she set it down again. "The Cardinal finally thought to look here, too, perhaps?"

"Perhaps." He turned slowly, to check that nothing had been left untouched. "We will look anyway."

Susanna began sifting through the straw from the mattress.

She found a crumpled piece of paper and the spy snatched it from her, read it, and threw it down in disgust. Out of interest, Susanna picked it up and saw with shock that it was written in her father's hand.

A letter from her father to Jens, yet she was still waiting for a letter after nearly two months.

It was the first page of the letter only, and covered the pleasantries and greetings. Her eyebrows rose as she read her father's boasting of her position at the English court, and the fine work her brother Lucas was doing in Germany.

She began to look for the second page, carefully checking under the straw and lifting the broken bed.

The spy grunted in approval.

At last, Susanna sat back in frustration. "It is gone."

"It seems to be. If it was ever here."

She had to remember they were talking about the Mirror, not her father's letter. She folded the page she had and slipped it into the money pouch hanging from her belt. "What makes you think it wasn't here?"

"If it was, it was in the last thing they smashed, which doesn't seem likely. Come. The Comte is waiting." He held out a hand to her, but she got to her feet herself.

As they walked back through the warren of passages, each step seemed heavier than the last. She wondered if Parker was awake. Wondered if the boys had made it back.

Wondered if the Comte would let her live.

It felt as if she were walking to her execution.

---

Parker pulled himself up onto the dock at Westminster, every joint aching with cold, and stiff from sitting still in the small boat.

"The tide is going out," the boatman said, the first time he'd spoken since Parker hailed him.

Parker turned back. "My pardon?"

"Low tide. If you want to get downstream later, you won't be able to get past Old Swan unless you shoot the bridge."

Parker nodded and the boatman pushed off.

Westminster Palace loomed large and black, almost entirely unlit. There would only be servants and guards here, and precious few of them. He hoped to God he had guessed right; Susanna might not be here at all.

"Sir?" The whisper came from the right, from behind a stack of crates.

"Eric?" The relief that surged through him made him weak-kneed. But the pain and the exhaustion could lay claim to him later. He needed all his strength.

Eric ran around the crates, stood trembling before him. "The Comte. He's waiting for her farther in." He looked over his shoulder. "I don't know where the assassin is. He wasn't with them. Peter Jack and Harry thought he might be hidden out of sight, watching." He stepped closer to Parker. "I expect to feel his bolt through my back every step I take."

"Where are Harry and Peter Jack?"

"Watching the Comte. Come with me."

Parker warmed up as he jogged after Eric. The boy slipped between two smaller buildings, and Parker followed him along the narrow path that ran behind the houses toward the palace.

Eric whistled, the high, fluting call of a robin redbreast, and was answered in kind.

Harry appeared, crouched low against a wall, and Parker bent low and ran across the open ground to join him, Eric right beside him.

"The Comte is hiding behind a line of hedges over there." As Harry pointed, Parker saw he had been beaten. His eye was swollen and there was dark bruising along his jaw.

"Where is Peter Jack?"

"Watching from the corner of the palace. We don't know where my lady went in, or where she'll come out. I can't imagine she's in there alone, but if the assassin is with her, we didn't see him."

Parker slipped his knives out of his sleeves. "He may be on his way here, but he was at the Comte's mansion an hour ago."

"So we don't know who is with her." Harry closed his eyes.

"What do we do now?" Eric tugged at Parker's sleeve, and Parker could see the boy was at the end of his endurance. He'd run on foot from the Comte's mansion all the way out here, then kept watch even though he feared the assassin could be watching him.

"You and Harry stay here, keep an eye on the Comte. I'm going to look for Susanna in the palace."

"Just walk through the palace entrance?" Eric seemed startled.

Parker rose up. "I am its Keeper. The Comte is on *my* territory here."

# 35

*And to make this quite clear I say that I consider those who are able to support themselves by their own resources who can, either by abundance of men or money, raise a sufficient army to join battle against any one who comes to attack them; and I consider those always to have need of others who cannot show themselves against the enemy in the field, but are forced to defend themselves by sheltering behind walls.*

—Machiavelli, The Prince, *chapter 10*

The Comte walked out from the gardens, into the thin light that spilled from behind Susanna as she stepped out of the side door.

Her watcher took a grip on her arm, as if afraid she would bolt.

He was right to be afraid.

"Well?" In the dim light, Susanna could see that the Comte's face was eager, his hopes high.

He would strike back all the harder because of it when he learned the bad news.

"Wolsey got there first." The spy kept wisely out of the Comte's reach as he spoke softly in French.

"What?" The Comte went very still.

"If it is any consolation, I do not think he found anything in the room. Every piece was smashed. The Mirror is elsewhere."

"I thought . . ." The Comte raised both hands to his forehead, massaged the sides. "Where else could that damned *diamantaire* have left it?"

Susanna said nothing. She had not been addressed, and if the Comte's spy had not had such a tight hold on her, she would have tried to slip away.

"You." The Comte pointed a finger at her. "You knew Jens; where would he have hidden it?"

She sighed. "The man I knew came to dinner with my family and laughed with us. He played with me as a child, and sent me presents on my birthday." She looked straight at the Comte. "The man I met in London a few days ago tried to kill me with his chisel in a dark alley. I do not know where he would have hidden it."

"That is the problem exactly." The Comte spun in rage, his hands fists. "He thought he was for the Tower at any moment. It unbalanced him. He could have thrown it in the Thames, for all I know."

"Perhaps he did."

The voice came from behind her, and suddenly the grip on her arm fell away. The spy made a faint sigh as he crumpled to the ground.

"Parker." She blinked, and he was beside her.

He looked the worse for wear, his face white, with a dark bruise on his forehead. He did not move in his usual, easy way—his whole body was clenched tight with pain.

But there was no mistaking the gleam of steel in one hand, a club in the other. There was a set to his jaw that said he would bear the pain and more; his focus was entirely on the Comte.

"The way Jean spoke of you today, I thought you were near death, my friend." The Comte took a step back.

"Obviously not." Parker lifted a hand, a signal of some sort, and three guards stepped from the shadows. "I think the Comte has turned in here by mistake. Please escort him out onto the road."

The Comte bowed, but Susanna saw the flash of hatred in his eyes. He gestured to one of the guards to lead the way, and walked off without a backward glance, leaving his spy lying unconscious on the ground.

"Madame." Parker turned and crushed her to him, and she let herself be enveloped.

"You should be abed," she whispered.

He barked out a laugh. "Aye, but my betrothed goes out and stirs up trouble in the middle of the night." He paused a moment. "I listened a little to the talk before I stepped forward. Am I right that the French found nothing?"

"They were looking in the wrong place."

"It's a pity we don't know the right place." He released her a little, and ran a hand over her hair.

She smiled up at him. "But we do."

———

They went home.

The Jewel Tower was locked, and Eric, Peter Jack, and

Harry had the stark-eyed look of war veterans. Parker could barely stand straight himself.

Susanna's throat was a rainbow of bruises, and there were dark circles beneath her eyes. She had done more than he could believe in one day. Formidable things.

The Mirror could stay where it was. It seemed they were the only ones who knew it was there.

*If* it was there.

When they came to the house on Crooked Lane, he saw Eric actually weep with relief.

A cold rage gripped Parker. There would be an accounting for this day. For this whole week.

Mistress Greene opened the door as soon as his boot took the first step.

Eric ran to her, and she grabbed him up and dragged him into the kitchen, tiny sobs escaping her.

Parker let Harry and Peter Jack follow them in, and then turned to hold out a hand for Susanna.

She let him pull her up the last step, and stood close and warm in his arms.

"You must have a strong longing for bed." Her voice still caught on a rasp, and his fists clenched her cloak. He wished he had given in to temptation and used his knife on Jean's throat earlier. An injury for an injury.

He kept his voice even. "Aye. And you."

She nodded against his shoulder, holding tight and burrowing in deep.

"What did Norfolk say to you? Jean said he was having you followed."

He could tell she did not want to answer, because she went very still.

"What did he say?" He rubbed her shoulders, and slowly, she relaxed again.

"He saw the Comte talking to me in the Privy Chamber when I went to speak to the King. He said he'd use that, use the fact that others had seen, too, to build a case of treason against me if I got in the way of his plans to bring down Wolsey. He said he would fabricate as much as he could get away with."

The rage burned even colder, and Parker held her a little tighter.

"This is going to get worse, isn't it?" she whispered.

"Yes." He looked up to the stars that showed through the patches of cloud. "Worse for them."

# 36

*So it happens with fortune, who shows her power where valour has not prepared to resist her, and thither she turns her forces where she knows that barriers and defences have not been raised to constrain her.*

—Machiavelli, The Prince, *chapter 25*

They slept late, and it was almost midday before their barge bumped up against the dock at Westminster.

As Susanna accepted Parker's hand, she looked up at the Jewel Tower in anticipation and fear.

They walked to the entrance in silence; took the stairs to the room where they had spent time with Thomas Wyatt only a few days ago.

It felt like years.

Parker stopped, sudden and quiet, and Susanna saw Wyatt outside the room, papers strewn across his desk, eyes closed, his golden locks all wild about him.

"Wyatt." Parker drew them closer, and Susanna looked down at the desktop. He had been writing poetry, she saw in a brief glimpse before Wyatt's eyes snapped open and he scooped the pages to him.

"What?" He seemed not to recognize them at first, then relaxed back into his chair. "You."

Parker tried the door to the room, and when he found it locked, extended his palm to Wyatt.

As he took keys from his pocket, Wyatt kept his gaze on Parker. "You have Wolsey in a grip of dread. He looks as if he has not slept. He attended lunch in the Privy Chamber yesterday, which he never does. Many thought it to ingratiate himself with the King after their fight the night before over you. Halfway through the meal, a servant came with a message and Wolsey left. He looked as if he were ailing."

Susanna smiled. Most likely Wolsey's men had sent word that she had rescued Parker from his cell.

Wyatt was watching her, and his eyes widened. "You seem to know something of it, my lady."

"She was the cause of it." Parker turned the key and pushed open the door. "Give us the inventory, Wyatt."

Wyatt drew open a drawer in the desk and pulled out the roll of parchment. Susanna took it and stepped into the room after Parker, Wyatt behind her.

There it was. She looked at the small note Jens had made in the margin and nodded, her pulse racing.

"Box 136."

Parker began searching for it, and Wyatt joined him. Susanna thought about where Jens would put the box, especially knowing there would be a search after the Mirror was discovered missing. She sat on the large chest in the center of the room, looking up and around as she turned on it.

Then she stilled.

Stood.

And opened the chest she was sitting on.

"What is it?" Wyatt turned her way. "That is empty: we use it only to sit on."

Susanna ignored him and lifted the lid. "Box 136." Even though she whispered it, her voice was audible in the silent room. She lifted out a small casket, amazed at the weight of it.

The box was unlocked, and she flipped the lid open with a finger.

The sun caught the stone, making a thousand rainbows dance on the walls. Susanna lifted the piece out and the diamond covered the whole of her palm; the pear-shaped pearl dangling below it caressed her wrist, smooth as silk.

She lifted her eyes and caught Parker's gaze. He saluted her with a tip of his head, and she smiled back at him.

Dumbstruck, Wyatt opened his mouth, closed it again, and then sank to the floor on his knees. "How? How did you puzzle it out?"

"Jens left a clue on this inventory." Susanna set the jewel back into its box. "It was in French, and I only realized later what it could mean."

"What did it say?"

"Chased piece, 136."

"I saw that." Wyatt pulled himself to his feet. "I thought he was talking about an engraved piece." He dusted his knees. "As was his intention."

Parker held out his hands and Susanna placed the casket in them.

"What will you do now?" Wyatt looked at the small box as if it were a snake. "Wolsey cannot be called to account for this. It never left the Jewel Tower."

"I will take it to the King." Parker snapped the lid shut.

"And then? Wolsey will get away with this." Wyatt ran hands through his already wild hair, making it stand more on end. It caught the light and he looked like some wild sprite, elemental and beautiful. Susanna was suddenly sure his poetry was magnificent.

"Not if I can help it." Since last night, the shutters had come down over Parker's eyes and darkness seemed to swirl around him.

She had seen him like this before, and she knew the signs.

He was about to wreak havoc.

———

Anticipation hummed through Parker as the sailboat navigated downriver from Westminster to Bridewell.

The casket was nestled on Susanna's lap. Wolsey would likely flee the room if he saw what Parker was bringing for the King today.

And Norfolk . . . Well, Norfolk would need to be handled carefully.

The boatman let out a little more sail and they flew faster on the water. He caught Parker watching him and grinned.

Parker heard the buzz of vibration as something flew through the air past his ear. In a soundless movement, the boatman let go of the ropes and fell into the water, a bolt through his eye.

Parker twisted to see Jean cranking the next bolt into his bow. He stood dangerously forward in a boat behind them, balancing himself with a foot against the prow, ready to take aim again.

"Hold the casket over the water."

Susanna dragged her gaze from the spot where the boatman floated in the river and lifted shocked eyes to his.

"The casket—hold it out over the side of the boat!"

She scrambled to the edge of the boat and thrust the casket out, holding it with both hands. The weight of it took her by surprise again and it dipped dangerously low to the water. She lifted it a little higher.

Parker turned to see if Jean had gotten the message, and saw he had. The assassin had lifted his crossbow so it was pointing to the sky.

"You found it." His words carried across the water.

His voice was filled with wonder, and Parker realized Jean hadn't known they had found the Mirror until now. He had come to kill them.

"Shoot either one of us, and Susanna drops the casket into the Thames."

Jean set his bow in the boat behind him and lifted both

hands. "I will not shoot." He sat and his boat kept pace with theirs, to the right and slightly back.

"What now?" Susanna pitched her voice low.

"Now he thinks he has only to wait for us to land, before that crossbow is in his hands again." Parker took up the ropes of the boat and trimmed the sail, trying to remember the tricks he had learned in his youth.

Susanna drew the casket in. "This is heavy." She sat right up against the side of the boat and put the small wooden box in her lap. "What do we do about Jean?"

The wind tugged back against his hold on the ropes, and the boat surged forward. It was an old boat but well made, and it seemed to skim just above the water, rather than on top of it.

"The tide is out." Parker pulled the sail again. "That means the bridge will be unpassable."

"So we are trapped. We have to dock at Old Swan, and Jean knows it." Susanna spoke calmly, and he was struck again by her courage.

He watched her, grim. "Not if we shoot the bridge."

She did not answer him, and turned away toward the left bank. Bridewell was coming up around the bend, their original destination, but Jean would have a bolt through each of them and the casket in his hand if they tried to dock there. It was too crowded and busy for a quick getaway.

At last Susanna swung back, her face set. "We shoot the bridge, then."

He nodded. Turning his head to check where Jean and his boatman were, he saw they were gaining a little.

The bow was in Jean's hands, and Parker frowned. What was the Frenchman up to?

He understood when the first bolt went through the sail. Jean was trying to slow them down. After the first shock of realizing they had the Mirror, he had had a chance to think. And he knew they were as unwilling to see the Mirror in the Thames as he was.

"Sit low." His call to Susanna came just as another bolt sliced through the sail, punching a hole through the middle of it.

Susanna slipped off the bench onto the boat bottom and balanced the casket on the edge of the boat. A nice reminder to Jean of their advantage in this. Then she lowered it over the side, and skimmed it on top of the water.

Parker had to stop himself from calling to her to bring it back up.

"Stop!" Jean's eyes were on the casket. He set the bow down again, and then lifted his gaze to Susanna. Parker saw a look pass between them.

There was a respect in Jean's eyes; determination in the set of Susanna's mouth.

They were coming up to Queenhithe now, the dock busy with the loading and unloading of grain, and up ahead, a line of boats waiting out the low tide.

This low on the river, Parker could see the churn and ripple of water at the bridge arches, and he wondered what the drop would be. Last time he'd shot the bridge, it had been a man's height—but an experienced boatman had taken him through.

Susanna's face was composed. She was ready for what was to come. She had the casket on her lap again, clutched with both hands.

"You come before that damned jewel." He risked a look behind him to check Jean's progress, then back. "Don't hold on to it if it means you won't be safe."

She nodded, and looked over her shoulder to see the bridge coming up. The boats waiting the tide out were clustered to the left, near Old Swan, and Parker swung the boat right to go around them.

The tension in the ropes was more flaccid since Jean had put two holes through the sail, but the boat still moved sweet and true through the water. Parker heard calls and whistles from the boatmen as they rounded the little fleet, then cries of alarm as they headed straight for the arches.

"Wait!" Jean's shout carried over the hiss and roar of the churning water coming up, and Parker twisted on the bench toward him.

The assassin had his bow in his hand, and deliberately dropped it into the water. "Don't do it. I won't shoot."

Too late.

The current gripped the craft and spun it, and Susanna cried out as she was thrown across the boat.

The box flew from her hands, sailing over the side.

As they were sucked through the arch he heard a scream, and the last thing he saw before the darkness of the tunnel was Jean leaping into the Thames.

# 37

*Because the King of France would have made a thousand excuses, and the others would have raised a thousand fears.*

—Machiavelli, The Prince, *chapter 25*

ell was noise and wet and darkness, with an inexorable force hauling them through the long arch toward the light at the end.

Susanna's hair flew about her face as they shot through the water.

"Brace!"

Parker's call was unnecessary. She was on the floor of the boat, gripping the bench so tight her hands ached. She lifted her head as the vessel went airborne, saw the foam and the spray all around her.

The boat dropped, smacking down hard on the water. The floor vibrated under the blow, shaking her like a leaf in an autumn wind.

The front dipped, held there a moment . . . and then rose up again. The current turned them in a slow and lazy pirouette, once, twice, until Parker had control of the craft again.

In silence, he took them to the closest dock and helped her off.

There in broad daylight, he bent his head and kissed her eyes, her cheeks, her mouth; holding her close and tight.

Her legs were weak and she let him hold her up.

"I am sorry that after all that, we lost the Mirror." He twined his fingers through her hair.

She looked up. "I hope not."

"It flew from your hand—"

Shaking her head, she fumbled for her money pouch. "The box flew from my hand." She lifted up the Mirror, glittering and dazzling in its brilliance. "This didn't."

---

For safekeeping Parker sent Susanna to Bridewell, into the nest of vipers, where they would least likely expect her. Hiding her in plain sight.

There were many things to accomplish, and too many powerful men who meant her harm.

She took her paints, and Gertrude Courtenay met her in the Queen's outer chambers.

"The princess is here today, so the Queen hopes you can begin to paint her picture."

Susanna curtsied and waved Parker farewell, but he didn't

leave until he saw her safely escorted into the Queen's inner rooms.

The Mirror weighed heavily in the inside pocket of his cloak, and he moved toward the King's chambers with the knife up his sleeve loosened and ready.

Wolsey had left the palace that morning, he had been told, and Parker could only think it was a strategic retreat.

He could prove nothing against Wolsey, and Wolsey knew that.

But the Cardinal could run as far and as fast as he liked. Parker clenched a fist. He would make certain Wolsey paid his account in this.

The guards at the Privy Chamber fell back and opened the door for him, and Parker strode into the room. It was full of courtiers, milling and sniping, but the King was not present.

"He's in his closet." Will Somers peered at Parker as if inspecting a strange new creature. Then the Fool put a hand on his arm. "I saw your lady the other night. Is she well?"

"Well enough." He pulled his arm back, but Somers kept his grip.

"She did not look well at the time, and I would warn you that after she left, the Duke of Norfolk began all manner of whispers about her."

Parker cut his gaze to the corner where he'd noticed Norfolk earlier, and saw the Duke was watching him. Watching the exchange. "So I heard."

"Ah? You know?" Somers dropped his hand and smiled,

the gleefully evil smile of a gargoyle. "I look forward to your retaliation."

Parker did not bother with an answer. He dismissed Norfolk with a jerk of his head and made for the closet. Somers's chuckle followed him.

The guards at the closet looked set to deny him, but at the last moment opened the door. Parker stepped into the room and stood just within, and saw the King sitting with his secretary.

He seemed pleased with the interruption.

"News, Parker?"

"Aye."

Henry waved the secretary out, and when they were alone, Parker reached into his pocket and drew out the Mirror.

Henry stared at the jewel, then reached out his hand and took it. "I'd forgotten how magnificent it is."

"It has cost many lives to get it back." Parker thought of the boatman just an hour ago, of Norfolk's hapless spies. Of Jens. He rubbed his shoulder. "Too many."

"Who did this, Parker?" Henry ran a thumb over the facets. "Who?"

"I have no solid proof. And those who could give the proof will not, because it implicates them, too."

"Then a name without proof. I trust you have it right."

"You will not like it." Restless, Parker walked to the fire, and then to the window. He had always been truthful with the King, but this truth could sink him. Henry would not want to hear it.

Henry was quiet.

Parker turned and saw he was watching him, a look in his eye that was hard to decipher.

"I hear many things these days I do not like. I will not kill the messenger."

Parker braced himself. "Wolsey."

Whatever the King had expected, this was not it. His mouth gaped, and he stared at Parker with unblinking eyes. He tried to speak; cleared his throat. "Why?" The word came out on a croak.

"He arranged it months ago, when the King of France had an alliance with Rome. The Emperor has promised often to advance Wolsey as pope, and has failed to carry out his promise each time. Wolsey thought to bribe the French with the Mirror of Naples to do it this time."

"But the alliance is over now."

"Aye." Parker kept his eyes on the King, watching for a change in mood. "When the deal went sour, Wolsey tried to stop it. But the man he'd hired to take the jewel had already done so and hidden it, and Wolsey could not find where he'd put it."

"Wolsey made some accusations against you the other night. How do I know this is not your retaliation against that?"

Parker shrugged. "You do not. The French could confirm it, but they will not. They don't want the finger pointed at them in this."

Henry rubbed stiff fingers against his forehead. "He is my right hand."

"Aye. And I have no real proof. There is nothing to be done. But you asked me, and I told you. Wolsey did this. And the French cleaned up after him, killing all who could stand witness against either of them." He moved again, too restless to do anything else.

"This does not sit well." Henry rose, too, and joined Parker at the window. "What is your recommendation?"

"At the very least, wear the jewel soon. Show it is in your possession."

"Aye. That is good counsel." Henry lifted it to the light. "There is a spectacle with emissaries from Venice tonight. I will wear it then." He moved the Mirror this way and that, creating rainbows. "I would go to war with France, but Wolsey insists we have no money. Each day that the Emperor delays in sending word that he will support me in an invasion bodes worse for a swift attack. Retrieving the Mirror from France's grasp is at least some show of strength."

Parker said nothing. The sun shining through the window warmed his face. For a moment he longed for nothing more than his bed, and he closed his eyes.

"You look the worse for wear, Parker. This"—Henry flicked the pearl hanging below the diamond—"has come at a personal cost."

"Aye." Parker did not see the point in denying it. "To me and mine."

"You will not go unrewarded."

Parker shrugged. He would take what was given to him and he would use it, but he had never pushed for any favor from the King, save one—Susanna Horenbout's hand. And he had been given it.

Henry laughed. "You inspire me always to surprise you with my generosity, given how lightly you take it, and how little you seem to want it."

"I do what I do out of loyalty, not out of greed." Parker saw no leverage in pretending otherwise.

"Aye. And because of that, although it pains me, I believe you about Wolsey. But I have use for him yet, and no good will come of my turning on him with so little evidence. The nobles will squabble with each other and petition me for his offices and his wealth, and in return, they will not give me half as much as he does in terms of work. No matter what Wolsey may have done now, he can work from sunrise until long after sunset on my business, and I will always be in his debt for that."

Parker knew he spoke true. But if the Cardinal was going to get away with this in the short term, perhaps a more personal visit was in order.

"Any other trouble?" the King asked.

"One favor I will ask of you." Parker thought of Norfolk, lurking in his corner outside.

"Aye?" Henry waited for him, arms crossed over his chest.

"Do not pay heed to any rumors or whispers from Norfolk about your painter. My betrothed is as loyal as I am."

"I know it, but what is the story here?" Parker had seen that gleam in Henry's eyes before. The monarch was insatiably curious.

"Norfolk could have alerted you to the Mirror's disappearance some weeks ago, but he held back, trying to find a way to ensnare Wolsey and ruin him. The French almost laid hands on the jewel because of it.

"Norfolk threatened my betrothed with the Tower if she retrieved the Mirror before he could find some evidence against Wolsey. It is she you have to thank for the return of this jewel. She worked out where it was hidden."

Henry's lips thinned. Parker knew the King did nothing to stop the vicious rivalry in his court, thinking it provided him with a self-sustaining system of checks and balances, but sometimes the bitterness between the power factions was not to his advantage. "So noted. There will be no Tower in your lady's future."

"Good." Parker bowed, and Henry sat again at his desk.

"Call that damnable secretary back as you leave."

Parker stepped into the Privy Chamber and caught Norfolk's eye. The Duke was watching the door, a fox hunkered down outside the chicken roost.

Parker sent him a long, slow smile, and watched Norfolk take a step back.

Turnabout was fair play.

# 38

*And here it must be noted that such—like deaths, which
are deliberately inflicted with a resolved and desperate
courage—cannot be avoided by princes.*

—Machiavelli, The Prince, *chapter 25*

Hampton Court Palace was magnificent.

Parker had not been to see the progress of Wolsey's
project for a long time, and he was astonished at the beauty
and elegance of the building.

It was a palace for a monarch, not a priest; for a king, not
his administrator. Given the relatively cramped conditions of
Bridewell, Wolsey had succeeded in upstaging his master in
this.

Workmen were still busy around the back. Parker heard
the clang of iron on stone, and the calls of men to each other.
He wondered what Wolsey thought to do once the place was
finished. How could he entertain here, do business here, without showing up his monarch?

It was madness.

He walked around the side of the building, and stepped through a door muddy with the tracks of workmen.

As he moved toward the front of the palace, the rooms became finer and more finished. No expense had been spared, and the detail was remarkable.

Wolsey had turned his considerable talents of organization to creating perfection, and had almost achieved it.

Parker heard the murmur of voices ahead and moved toward the sound, turning a corner to see two servants walking away with trays of used plates.

Large double doors sat closed to his right, and he knew whom he would find behind them. A laugh came, light and feminine, and Parker stepped back as the door opened.

A woman slipped out, her face smoothing to neutral as she closed the door and followed the servants.

Alone at last.

His knife neatly in his grip, Parker eased the door open and stepped inside. The light outside was fading, and the lantern on Wolsey's desk and the fireplace provided a gentle glow that threw the rest of the room in shadow.

Wolsey stood before the fire, his back to the door, and Parker stood quietly, waiting for Wolsey to sense him.

The moment he did, Wolsey spun, staggering a little as he put himself off balance. "Parker!" He moved to his desk, gripping the edge for support. "Why are you here?"

"You know why. And my stay under the Fleet is only a part of it."

Parker leaned back against the door.

Wolsey's gaze flicked to him and away. "You have no proof against me."

Parker tilted his head. "I don't need proof. Just as you don't seem to need a court for the Fleet."

Wolsey felt behind him, knocking stacks of paper on his desk as he blindly fumbled for something. "The King will not countenance an injury to me."

"I think the King will not so much as raise an eyebrow."

Wolsey's skin was suddenly stark against the dark color of his robes. "You pointed the finger at me?"

"I told the King all I know, and you were most certainly mentioned." Parker fingered the hilt of his knife. "Having possession of the Mirror when I told the tale added no little weight to my words."

Wolsey gave up trying to find whatever it was he sought, and lifted a hand to his mouth. "You found the Mirror?"

Parker smiled.

"The King did not believe you, or it would not be you here, but some sheriff to take me to the Tower." Wolsey spoke slowly, weighing each word and finding them to his liking. He smiled back, his hands shaking with relief.

"The King did not want to believe me. Whether he did or not, I will leave to you to discover." Parker stepped forward. "In fact, I think your punishment can be wondering when the King will no longer find you useful enough to forget you put your own ambition before his. One day, his temper will fray too far. The day he sees this palace of yours, perhaps?"

Wolsey frowned. "You could be lying. What is to say you even spoke with the King at all?"

"Come to Bridewell tonight." Parker turned and put his hand on the door. "The King will be wearing the Mirror, and you can see how well he likes you."

"Perhaps I will." Wolsey spoke boldly, but Parker could hear the fear beneath.

"If you ever touch or speak with my betrothed again," Parker said as he opened the door, "if you ever send thugs after me, or attempt any harm to any of my servants or family, I will kill you."

"You insolent dock rat." Wolsey drew himself tall. "I have more power than you will ever have."

"All your power is worth nothing with a knife between your ribs. And if you come near me or mine again, that is exactly what you will have."

———

Susanna watched the Venetian emissaries watch the pageant. Or rather, pretend to watch it while their gaze was drawn elsewhere.

To the King.

He was always a striking presence, but tonight, in his dark blue velvet doublet embroidered with gold thread and picked out with jewels, he looked magnificent. And from his shoulder hung the Mirror of Naples.

In the glow of a thousand candles, it took her breath away, and she understood why it was at the center of the last few days' madness.

She noticed someone else looking at the Mirror, with an intensity and focus that spoke of obsession.

As if he felt her gaze, he turned to her, and for a terrible moment she and the Comte stared into each other's eyes. There was hatred there; a pure, cold fury.

Parker put a hand on her shoulder, and she cast a quick glance up at him. When she turned back to the Comte, he was gone.

"He would like to kill me," she said. She couldn't help the shiver that slithered through her.

"I have Harry and Peter Jack asking questions along the river to see if Jean drowned in the Thames this morning or not." Parker kept looking for the Comte, but from his expression, Susanna guessed the French nobleman had disappeared.

"The Comte will kill me himself if he can. He would not go running to Jean."

Parker lifted the back of his hand to her cheek and stroked it. "You are becoming too like me, my lady. There are those all about you who wish you harm."

Susanna laughed, a weary sound. It had been a long day. "Can we take our leave?"

Parker gave a nod, and took her with him to say his farewells to the King.

Norfolk was standing with Henry, and Susanna went cold, the conversation she had had with Norfolk in his house clear in her mind. The Duke was out to ruin her.

"Your Majesty, it has been a busy day. We will depart." Parker bowed low to the King and dipped his head in Norfolk's direction.

"I have been busy since our meeting earlier, Parker. You will find you are no longer my Yeoman of the Crossbows." Henry paused and looked sidelong at Norfolk.

Susanna squeezed Parker's hand, but he did not look shocked or even concerned.

"You are now my Yeoman of the King's Robes."

Norfolk hissed, the sound as loud and enraged as a boiling kettle. "That is an elevation indeed."

Parker had been powerful before, but this further responsibility elevated him among his peers in the Privy Chamber. It was an honor from the king.

"You are most generous, Your Majesty." There was amusement in Parker's voice, and Henry let out a deep laugh.

Norfolk stood beside them, white-lipped.

"Take your leave with my blessing. I know this has been a busy day." Henry fingered the glittering jewel at his shoulder. "I gather some thanks are owed you, Mistress Horenbout, for the day's work."

Susanna curtsied.

"As it happens, I have a question for Mistress Horenbout." Norfolk stared at her and Parker, his eyes narrowed.

"Be very careful which questions you ask Mistress Horenbout, lest some questions be leveled at you." Henry spoke softly, his full attention on Norfolk, and Norfolk took a step back.

"Norfolk." Parker gave a curt nod of his head, and Susanna did not even dip.

The Duke bowed to the King and withdrew, his steps unsteady.

Parker drew her away, taking her trembling hands in his.

"Will that hold him?" she whispered.

"For a while."

Susanna came to a dead stop, her eyes on the door. Cardinal Wolsey stood in the entrance, his official robes on and a parchment in his hands.

"Your Majesty." His call cut through the talk and laughter, and the company went quiet.

Henry stepped into the space that had opened up on the floor between him and his chancellor.

"My lord chancellor."

"This is my plan of completion for Hampton Court Palace." He held the parchment up. "If all goes well, it will be finished shortly." He paused. "Today, as I surveyed the work, I realized that in my enthusiasm to build a fine place to which I could invite my monarch, I have created more than a humble servant needs. When the last brick is laid, and the last room furnished, I will cede ownership to you."

It was done more publicly than the King would like, Susanna guessed. But for a man facing possible imprisonment, a man who knew not his standing with the King, it was necessary for as many to witness his massive act of generosity as possible.

"It was merely a matter of time," Parker breathed in her ear. "I saw Hampton Court today, and if Wolsey hadn't given it to him, Henry would have taken it. Wolsey knows it. And after all his cards tumbled down today, this was quick thinking on his part. I cannot begin to imagine what it has ripped out of him to give up Hampton Court."

"If he loved it, this is perhaps an apt reckoning for what he has done."

Parker shook his head. "Henry will never forgive him for a betrayal. There will be an accounting, but Henry will let Wolsey work himself to the bone before he brings down the ax."

"Will he really rid himself of Wolsey? He does not look as if he would even consider it."

Susanna saw the King take the architect's plan from Wolsey and hold out his hand for Wolsey to kiss. Henry's face was jovial and his eyes danced.

"I am sure of it." Parker walked with her out of the room, away from false smiles and insincere offers. "Wolsey is a dead man walking."

# 39

*And whereas I have sought to make them my enemies,*
*because I believed that war with them would conduce to*
*my power and glory, thou hast every inducement to*
*make friends of them, because their alliance will bring*
*thee advantages and security.*

—Niccolò Machiavelli, The Life of Castruccio Castracani of
Lucca (*translated by W. K. Marriott*)

The Comte was waiting for them as they stepped out of
Bridewell.

He made no attempt to hide himself and came forward
boldly, in full view of the guards at the door.

Parker reached for his sword, but the Comte lifted his
hands, palms outward, to show he held no weapons.

"May I ask, just from personal interest, where the Mirror
was hidden?" He came to a stop just out of sword reach.

"It was in the Jewel Tower, hidden in an unused box." Susanna spoke softly, and Parker thought there was some sympa-
thy for the Comte in her voice.

"Ah. What was Jens thinking?" The Comte's voice caught
and almost broke.

"I'm sorry. I truly am." Susanna made to move to him, but Parker held her back.

"Sorry? You *bitch*." The Comte moved suddenly, a knife magically in his hand.

Steel ground on steel as Parker's sword caught the blade and threw it back, flipping it out of the Comte's hand. It somersaulted in the air and landed with the high ting of metal on stone, then skittered away into the dark.

The guardsmen gave a shout, but Parker lifted a hand to show he had it under control.

He and the Comte stared at each other, breathing hard.

"I'd run for France if I were you." Parker's arms ached to thrust the sword home. "I would dearly love to kill you, but there would be repercussions and I do not intend to spend my time answering tiresome questions. The King knows your part in this, and things will not go well for you if you stay."

"I am away to Dover this very night." The Comte spoke tightly.

"Let me not delay you." Parker lifted his sword, ready for another strike.

"One word of warning." The Comte edged back. "Do not come to France, either of you. It will not go well for you."

He spun and strode to his horse.

Parker sheathed his sword.

Susanna was staring after the Comte, her face drawn. "He was in an impossible situation. I do not think his failure will do him any favors in France, either. I feel sorry for him."

Parker stared at her. "You are a mystery to me, my lady."

She turned to him. "Is it finally over now?"

"Aye." He drew her close. "It is over. Until the next time."

———————

The letter from home arrived the next day.

Susanna had been waiting so long for it, she let it sit on the table and simply looked at it. She had never thought she would miss her family as much as she did. Her mother particularly, but her father and her brother, too.

She'd left Ghent angry and disappointed in them, but her life had changed for the better in all ways since she'd come to London. Her father had done her the greatest favor to send her off.

She fingered the parchment, which was a little dirty from its journey, and finally took up a knife to break the seal.

The paper rolled open on her lap, and she saw it was in the beautiful hand of her father. He was not a scribe, but he formed his letters as if he were guided by angels.

She read the small, tight script once, then twice. Stood and went to stand by the fire. Happiness warred with anger, and even—she would admit—jealousy. Fury.

Even though the understanding had always been that this opportunity was temporary, now that he was taking it away, she realized how much this work meant to her. This life.

Being the visible artist, not the one who toiled in obscurity in the atelier.

"What is it?" Parker stood at the door, and she must have looked worse than she feared, because he came to her as if she had received some terrible news.

"I have a letter from my family." She pointed to it, lying on the small table beside her chair.

"And?" He made no move to reach for it.

"They are coming to England." She lifted her wrists to dab away the tears that were suddenly there. "My father has had enough of Margaret's administrators always paying him late. He is bringing my mother, and he and my brother Lucas will take over my work for the King."

Parker watched her with eyes that saw to her soul. "You do not want that."

She shook her head, afraid to speak. Afraid that the force of her desire to keep what she had would spill out into something uncontrolled.

"It seems to me you have other clients already, besides the King." He stroked her hair. "The Queen, and her ladies, are all clamoring for your pictures."

Susanna stilled. "Aye."

"And when you are married to me, your father cannot command you." Parker brushed away the last tear with his thumb.

"No. But you can." She looked up into his stark, beautiful face. They had never discussed what would happen with her work when she married him.

"You know my greatest wish is for your happiness." He kissed her forehead. "And if you want to paint, then that is what you will do."

She finally smiled, and framed his face with her hands, thinking of all the paintings she would do of him—an infinite number, showing every brilliant facet of him.

"Yes. That is exactly what I will do."

# AUTHOR'S NOTE

This is, of course, a work of fiction, but where possible I have kept to the events and facts of the time.

The story of how Henry VIII came to possess the Mirror of Naples is quite true, although what happened to the jewel is a mystery. Venetian ambassadors did describe a jewel worn by Henry that sounds very much like the Mirror, but after that it disappears from the record books.

Also true is the tale of Henry's headfirst dive into a ditch while hawking. The incident sent a ripple of alarm through the nobility on the question of succession, and Henry was very aware of this.

Wolsey's Amicable Grant is also fact. He was under pressure from the King to raise funds for a war with France. He bypassed Parliament and simply implemented the Grant, causing rioting and a massive backlash from the laity and nobility alike. He was forced to retract the Grant, a huge loss of face for him and the King.

In this book I have implied that Gertrude Courtenay, Countess of Devon, was the daughter of William Blount and his third wife, Ines de Benegas. However, I'd like to mention there is conflicting information on this fact. She is also listed as the daughter of William Blount and his second wife, Elizabeth Saye. All the sources were reputable, if at odds with one another, so as Alison Weir refers to Gertrude as being half Spanish in her book *Henry VIII: The King and His Court*, mentioning that her Spanish heritage made her very dear to Katherine of Aragon, I chose to keep her half Spanish for the purposes of this story.

The underground passage from St. Sepulchre's to Newgate Prison did exist. The one from St. Sepulchre's to the Fleet did not, except in my imagination.

Bartholomew Fair was the name of the underground dungeons that made up the most horrific cells of the Fleet, and some of the prisoners there were sent by the Star Chamber and by Wolsey himself. When the nobles and Henry acted against Wolsey and arrested him, one of the charges against him was sending people to the Fleet without due process.

And finally, "shooting the bridge" really was a pastime of the Thames boatmen with nerves of steel and a certain death wish. As the Thames flowed toward the sea and encountered the massive barrier of London Bridge, it was forced to slow and back up, like a dam. Because the river is tidal, when it was low tide the water on the seaward side of the bridge could be as much as six feet lower than the water on the source side. The pressure on the water as it forced its way through the bridge's arches was immense, and boatmen took their lives in their hands if they chose to navigate it.

Michelle Diener
www.michellediener.com

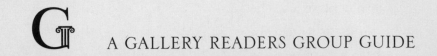

A GALLERY READERS GROUP GUIDE

# KEEPER OF THE KING'S SECRETS

## MICHELLE DIENER

# INTRODUCTION

In *Keeper of the King's Secrets*, a violent encounter between Susanna Horenbout and Master Jens of Antwerp, an old family friend and distinguished jeweller, soon becomes a race to prevent the theft of one of the King's most magnificent jewels—a theft that could plunge England into a war with France. After Susanna and her betrothed, courtier John Parker, learn of Jens's involvement in the disappearance of the King's beloved and controversial Mirror of Naples, they embark on a dangerous quest to find who is trying to steal the prized jewel—and which of Henry's inner court is working with an assassin to remove all those standing in his way. They tirelessly search for the jewel despite assassination attempts on their own lives, sinister plots against them devised by rival courtiers, and Parker's kidnapping by Cardinal Wolsey. Just when they have seemingly exhausted all avenues, Susanna solves the riddle of the jewel's hiding place. After one final struggle with the French assassin, Parker and Susanna successfully return the Mirror of Naples to King Henry VIII, thus averting the war with France Henry would have demanded had it been stolen and cementing Parker's status as one of the King's most loyal courtiers.

# TOPICS & QUESTIONS
# FOR DISCUSSION

1. Nearly all chapters begins with a quote from Machiavelli's *The Prince*. What do you think is the significance of these quotes? How did these quotes frame the chapters? Did they enhance your reading in any way? Why or why not?

2. *Keeper of the King's Secrets* is the second novel in a series. If you have not already read the first novel, *In a Treacherous Court*, did you find it difficult follow Susanna and Parker's story line? Are you interested in reading the first book? Explain.

3. King Henry VIII's mishap while hawking caused a ripple of concern among the royals and his court, while also drawing attention to Henry's lack of a male heir. Can you think of any recent incidents similar to the King's mud dive?

4. Both Parker and Susanna risk their lives and their social stations to find the King's jewel. Who do you think took the greater risks? Explain.

5. Of all the risks Susanna takes, her greatest one is dressing as a monk. Can you think of a modern-day crime equivalent to Susanna's impersonation?

6. Throughout the story, Parker and Susanna go to great lengths to not only find the Mirror, but also to protect one another. Do you think their partnership would've been more or less successful if they weren't engaged? How does their relationship aid their sleuthing dynamic? How does it hinder it?

7. Many characters, including the Comte and Queen Katherine, acknowledge their use of spies. With so many duplicitous characters, whom would you trust if you were Parker or Susanna? Whom would you trust the least?

8. From the Comte to Cardinal Wolsey to Norfolk, there are many antagonists in *Keeper of the King's Secrets*. Who do you think is the most conniving? The most sympathetic? Explain.

9. At the end of the story, Parker returns the Mirror of Naples to King Henry VIII, earning him a promotion and the King's favor. Do you predict Parker's promotion to Yeoman of the King's Robes will help ease tensions among his fellow courtiers, or cause him more troubles?

10. The Comte and Jean would argue that, although the Mirror of Naples was ultimately returned to King Henry VIII, it truly belongs to the French. Do you

agree? Were the Comte and Jean justified in wanting to take it back from England?

11. Readers are introduced to the deadly assassin in chapter three, but his identity remains a mystery for the majority of the story. Whom did you suspect the assassin was working for? Were you surprised to learn his identity and that the Comte employed him?

12. In an effort to placate King Henry VIII, Cardinal Wolsey publicly cedes ownership of Hampton Court to the King. Do you think this will make up for Wolsey's wrongdoings, or is he, as Parker predicts, a "dead man walking"? (p. 278)

# ENHANCE YOUR BOOK CLUB

1. Follow author Michelle Diener online. Visit her website: www.michellediener.com, "like" her Facebook page: www.facebook.com/pages/Michelle-Diener/196593580366013, and follow her on Twitter @michellediener.

2. Read the first book in the John Parker and Susanna Horenbout series, *In a Treacherous Court*. Perhaps select it as next month's book club read, or make it a reading challenge for your members.